CHRISTA WOLF was born in Landsberg, Warthe, in 1929. She studied German at Jena and Leipzig universities and has worked as an editor, lecturer, journalist and critic. She has written four novels: *Der Geteilte Himmel* (*The Divided Heaven*, 1963), *Nachdenken über Christa T.* (*The Quest for Christa T.*, 1968), *Kindheitsmuster* (*A Model Childhood*, 1977) and *Kein Ort, Nirgends* (*No Place on Earth*, 1979). She has also written short stories, essays and film scripts. Christa Wolf won the Heinrich Mann Prize in 1963, the National Prize in 1978, and the Georg-Büchner Prize in 1980. She was runner-up for the Nobel Prize in 1988.

Christa Wolf is a committed socialist of independent temper and for several years she was a member of the central committee of the East German Writers' Union. One of the most important writers to come out of Eastern Europe, Christa Wolf's writings reflect her preoccupation with the personal suppressions and official silences under Nazism, and with the events in Germany which followed the war.

In 1982 she was awarded a guest lectureship at the University of Frankfurt, where in May she gave a series of five 'Lectures on Poetics'. These related to studies and travels undertaken in Greece in 1980. The fifth 'lecture' was revised and expanded for publication as *Cassandra* (1983).

Virago publishes *A Model Childhood*, *No Place on Earth*, *Cassandra* and *The Quest for Christa T.*

Published by VIRAGO PRESS Limited 1989
20–23 Mandela Street, Camden Town, London NW1 0HQ
Published by arrangement with Farrar, Straus and Giroux Inc.
19 Union Square West, New York, N.Y. 10003
Originally published in German under the title
Störfall: Nachrichten eines Tages, copyright © 1987 by
Aufbau-Verlag Berlin und Weimar
English translation copyright © 1989 by
Farrar, Straus and Giroux

A CIP record for this title is available
from the British Library

Printed in Great Britain by
Cox & Wyman Ltd., Reading, Berkshire

Accident

Accident /

A Day's News

Christa Wolf

TRANSLATED BY
HEIKE SCHWARZBAUER
AND RICK TAKVORIAN

VIRAGO

Contents

*None of the characters in this book
is identical with a living person.
They have all been invented by me.*

C.W.

The connection between murder and invention has been with us ever since. Both derive from agriculture and civilization.
—CARL SAGAN

The long-sought missing link between animals and the really humane being is ourselves.
—KONRAD LORENZ

Accident

On a day about which
I cannot write in the present tense, the cherry trees
will have been in blossom. I will have avoided thinking, "exploded," the cherry trees have exploded, although only one year earlier I could not only think
but also say it readily, if not entirely with conviction.
The green is exploding. Never would such a sentence
have been more appropriate in describing the progress
of nature than this year, in this spring heat, following
the endlessly long winter. I knew nothing yet of the
warnings that would circulate much later about eating
the fruit, still invisible on the branches of the blos-
soming trees, on the morning when I was annoyed,
as I am every morning, by the bustlings of the neighbor's chickens on our freshly seeded lawn. White leg-
horns. The only good thing you can say about them
is that they react to my clapping and hissing with fear,
if also confusion. Still, most of them scattered in the

direction of the neighboring property. There's a good chance you'll be able to hang on to your eggs now, I thought spitefully, and I intimated to that authority who had begun early on to watch me alertly from a very distant future—a glance, nothing more—that I would not feel bound by anything anymore. Free to do and, above all, not to do as I pleased. That goal in a very distant future toward which all lines had run till now had been blasted away, was smoldering, along with the fissionable material in a nuclear reactor. A rare case . . .

Seven o'clock. Where you are now, brother, they begin punctually. You will have received your sedative shot half an hour ago. Now they have wheeled you from the ward into the operating room. Cases such as yours are usually the first to come under the knife. Now I imagine you feel a not unpleasant dizziness within your shaven head. The point is to prevent you from having any clear thoughts, any all too distinct feelings. Fear, for instance. Everything will be all right. This is the message that I'm transmitting to you as a focused beam of energy before they send you off into anesthetized sleep. Is it getting through? Everything will be all right. Now I summon up your head before my inner eye and seek out the most vulnerable spot where my thought can penetrate to your brain, which they are about to expose. Everything will be all right.

Since you can't ask, the kinds of beams I'm talking about are certainly not dangerous, dear brother. In a manner unknown to me, they traverse the poisoned layers of air without becoming infected. The scientific term is "contaminated." (I'm learning new words while you sleep, brother.) Sterile, completely sterile, they reach the operating room and your body, laid out helpless and unconscious, touching and knowing it within fractions of a second. Would know it even if it were more greatly disfigured than you claim it is. Effortlessly, they penetrate the powerful force field of your unconsciousness in search of the glowing, pulsating core. They retard the ebbing flow of your strength in a way which defies language. This you must rely on; that was the agreement. It still counts . . .

Although unsuspecting, we will not have been unprepared before receiving the news. Didn't it seem familiar to us? Yes, I heard someone inside me think: Why always only the Japanese fishermen? Why not us as well, for a change?

The Birds and the Test.

In the shower I let the water run down my body carelessly, without a second thought. Every single one of the countless experts who are now shooting up out of the ground like mushrooms (mushrooms! inedible this season!) has stated that the groundwater will not be endangered for a long, long time—if at all this time. In a clear brooklet. Singing in the shower is a bad habit. It also makes it difficult to hear the N E W S on my little Sanyo transistor radio chopped up and refashioned every hour into the news. The wayward trout. Fish for storing radioactive waste. Depending on his affiliation with one of the factions into which the public has predictably divided, whether he was an optimist or a pessimist, the expert would say: No. Under no circumstances will the core melt down. Or: But of course. Yes, yes. Even that eventuality cannot be excluded. In such a case, one would have to expect that phenomenon so graphically christened the China Syndrome by scientific wits. As long as the fire hasn't been extinguished—and, brother, you probably don't know that although it may be hard for graphite fires to start, we have been forced to learn that it is incredibly difficult to put them out—as long as the chain reaction continues, the reactor core can remain active, melting through the earth's core until it reemerges in the antipodes. Transformed, perhaps, but still glowing. Brother, do you remember lowering a beer bottle full of hydrochloric acid into the deep hole we dug in the sandpile in front of our house? It was conscientiously pasted over with warning labels, for we were confident that it would eat its way through to the antipodes. Do you remember the letter we wrapped watertight in cellophane and fastened to the neck of the bottle? And its contents? Brothers and sisters, that's what we called the antipodeans, and we urgently requested that they confirm receipt of our bottle post at the return address we had, naturally, included.

We used to be truly thankful whenever we were able to picture an idea. I couldn't dwell on the sudden notion of apologizing betimes to the antipodeans because I had to listen to what a radio announcer was asking a seemingly young expert who had kindly consented to join him in the studio. What was he doing with his children today, if he had any. He did. He said he had told his wife not to give the children any fresh milk, spinach, or salad. Also, to be on the safe side, not to let them play in the park or the sandbox. Just then, as I was squeezing some toothpaste onto my toothbrush, I heard someone say: So, it had to come to this!

The woman who had spoken was myself. Already on the third day, the test of how long I can be alone without starting to talk to myself had loosed the first chunks of audible monologue of this kind: So, now I'll just finish up the laundry and then that's it! Today was the fifth day spent under aggravated conditions and I began talking out loud to people who weren't there. You'd like that, wouldn't you! for example . . .

I don't know what kind of saw is used to cut open the cranium. They say one follows the seams which divide the skull into several segments. If we want to, the doctor told you to reassure you of the perfection of his technique, we can simply lift off the skullcap like any other cap and put it back on again later. But we don't even want to in your case. What they do want to do—fold up a single segment, more specifically, the one over the right temple—they will no doubt have done by now. Your brain matter lies exposed before them. It's getting time for me to concentrate on the hands of the surgeon. On his fingertips.

Impulses, for which there are no words. In the deepening wells of your unconsciousness, you shall be soothed. Are you suffering? What comes of the suffering which we cannot perceive . . .

Life as a series of days. Breakfast. Measuring out the coffee with the orange measuring spoon, turning on the coffee machine, savoring the aroma which envelops the kitchen. It hasn't yet occurred to me to try to be more strongly, more consciously aware of smells than I was before. I haven't yet realized that they will be lost to you. Losses cannot always be avoided, your doctor told you, but we try to keep them down to an absolute minimum. Boiling the egg for exactly five minutes, managing the trick, day in day out, in spite of the faulty egg-timer. Imperishable pleasures. The structure that carries life even through dead times. The cutting surface of dark Mecklenburg bread. Sliced kernels of rye. How and when are nuclids—another word I have just begun to learn—actually stored in kernels of grain? From my place at the kitchen table I could see the rich green of the immense field of grain behind our house, since the elderberry bushes were still bare. I was looking for the right word to describe its appearance. "Carpet." A green carpet. In the country, one always risks slipping into archaic imagery.

There wasn't a cloud in the sky that day. (Why did I think "dead time" just now?) In shadows cool and clean / Upon your carpets green / O sweet repose / O sweet repose. Songs which I haven't thought of for years, for decades. I informed that authority who was critically examining everything I ate that the eggs in my refrigerator had grown in the bellies of chickens before the accident. That they had been nourished with grass and seeds free of radiation and delivered right to the store, undated and guaranteed fresh. But not too fresh. Definitely not yesterday fresh.

O heavens' radiant azure.

According to what laws and how quickly does radioactivity spread, at best and at worst? Best for whom? And would those living in the immediate vicinity of the explosion have a slightly better chance if it were spread by a fair wind? If it were to ascend to the higher strata of the atmosphere and there set off on its journey as an invisible cloud? In my grandmother's day the word "cloud" conjured up condensed vapor, nothing more. Probably white and more or less prettily shaped—a picture in the sky to stir the imagination. Hurrying clouds like the ships of the sky / Oh, could I sail with you as you fly . . . You'd end up elsewhere. So said our grandmother, who never traveled anywhere unless she was evacuated. Why are we so addicted to travel, brother?

She would approve of the plum puree which we made ourselves last year, gasping beneath the burden of the harvest. She used to sprinkle hers with cinnamon; we chose not to. She, on the other hand, would never put an old crust of bread in Plaack's feed bucket, as I did after a brief moment's hesitation. She would use the stale bread to make her weekend bread soup with raisins, Polish style, the only one of her dishes I didn't like. It was sinful, she said—a word which she didn't otherwise use—sinful to throw away bread. I should remember that. Her only motto. Our grandmother was a modest woman, brother . . .

We're alive. Not exactly thriving at the moment as far as you're concerned, I'll grant you that. Your life is not exactly hanging by a silken thread, but certainly, I would think, by a suture. To think that a metallic instrument is just now skirting your cerebral membrane, presumably pushing aside the brain matter to make room for another instrument, with a microscope at its end . . . When we spoke on the telephone yesterday, I did not tell you what I recently saw on television: a computer, specially developed for operations on the human brain, programmed to make precise incisions down to one-hundredth of a millimeter. Less fallible than the human hand, they said. But we assured one another that the experience and finesse of your surgeon were one hundred percent reliable . . .

I stood still, in my hand the cup which I meant to put in the sink, and thought several times in a row as intensively as I could: You can rely on the experience and the finesse of your surgeon. On my way to the post office I stopped by old Weiss's place and was reminded once again that he looked rather more like a retired sea captain than a former stable hand. Former? he said. Fat chance. This year as well he would be tending his share of calves along with fishing in the Mildenitz and hunting for mushrooms in the pas-

tures by the village lake. Eighty-three was just a drop
in the bucket. But whether he would reach ninety like
his father . . . Wait a minute! said his wife as she came
out the door, pails of water in hand. Did he want to
die all of a sudden! The winter? Oh dear, she said, it
had been bad, very bad. Stoking the fire several times
a day, and the cold which had seemed to go on forever.
And not being able to go anywhere, not even to see
their son in town. There hadn't been a single bus
running anywhere, and "our father"—that's what she
called old Weiss her husband—wouldn't let her go
away overnight; she was a prisoner in her own house.
To which old Weiss placidly responded: Well, listen
to that! A woman belongs in the home. There, you
hear, said his wife, this had been going on for forty
years.

We should know the photographs, brother. I for
my part know only too well the series of photographs
of the refugee girl, the one who hides out with her
mother in a hut in some godforsaken village where
there is no other person but the farmworker's wife,
who then proceeds to die—almost simultaneously
with the girl's mother—of the typhoid fever which,
as we all know, found its way into the Mecklenburg
region right after the war, leaving this unknown girl
to be found by the owner of the hut, Weiss the stable
hand, upon his return from a POW camp: fresh as a
rose, without a friend in the world, timid, homeless,
no place left to turn but his hut. And that's the way
it goes, life, says Frau Weiss, in the same tone of voice

in which she would say: misery. And since I tend to
blame great misery on life's many small miseries, I
also tend to want to alleviate those small miseries and
think that one should try to organize a daily bus route.
Bah! said Herr Gutjahr, who likes to refer to himself
as the Secretary of the Post, there is no end of things
which ought to be done! He is proud of his foresight
in always having a little money tucked away should
somebody want to withdraw a certain amount, as I
do today. No problem, he says. Never a problem,
where there's a will there's a way, am I right or am
I right! And wasn't I afraid at night, being all alone
in the house. Of whom, I asked, to which he replied:
I guess you're right. I didn't mind hearing once again
how, as an invalid, he was driven out of Saxony only
to be stranded here; how he found wages and bread
for himself and his large family. I enjoyed drawing a
few Red Cross lottery tickets out of the long narrow
box—the million winner was well hidden, said Herr
Gutjahr, we both laughed—then I tore open the second ticket and held it out to him: five marks. Well,
I'll be damned, said Herr Gutjahr. He could not have
known how much I needed to win, superstitious as I
was on that day. And it didn't bother me in the least
that I then blew the five marks on five losers. Easy
come easy go, said Herr Gutjahr, while quickly at-
tending to a young colleague from the stable who
picked up a registered letter and left the small, bare
post room reeking of alcohol long after he had gone.
Alimony demands, said Herr Gutjahr. He was drink-

ing even more now, since the divorce. And the wife
wasn't all that much better, but, he demanded of me,
what woman took a beating lying down nowadays
from a husband who had had a few too many. Hardly
a one, said I, and couldn't resist asking what Herr
Gutjahr thought of the reactor accident. Oh well, he
said. What's done is done. And weren't these things
always blown way out of proportion? He, for his part,
had been in worse pickles in his life. And what more
could happen to a sick old man like himself. There
was a proverb for everything. What I don't know
won't hurt me. That was what he went by and he
didn't pay much attention to all that static on the
radio . . .

The operation could last three to four hours. Almost two hours have passed now and it is beginning
to become strenuous, brother, we sense that. By the
way, how does the time pass for you meanwhile?
What distance did you cover and in what region, while
I walked the four or five hundred steps from the post
office to our house. Something happened that caused
me to stop. Hey, brother. What's going on? Are you
letting yourself go? Now you listen to me. This is
1986. You are fifty-three years old. That which we
call life is far from over at such an age. There is more,
damn it, than just these dull, lived-out cells in you
which, bored to death and sentenced to eternal rep-
etition, can only do the one thing: build tumors. There
are also the others, millions, what am I saying! billions
of cells—will you stop turning away, not with such

a gesture and certainly not today—billions of cells, I say, sprightly, yes, particularly agile within the complicated structure of your brain, highly inquisitive, thirsting for experience, cells which you can't just let down and commit to death only because you don't happen to care, for the space of five minutes, what becomes of you. Dead tired, brother heart? At death's door? You're not usually one to exaggerate. Do you think, just because you're under general anesthesia, you can sneak out the back door? And no one is going to notice? It may be that your will to live is crumbling a bit. That's why this additional line has been installed, two heads are better than one, as our mother used to say (Take good care of your little brother!). But you've got to hang on. Don't let go, brother! Hang on. Yes, that's right. I'm going to pull a little bit now, I can see you already, ever closer, ever more clearly. Very close now. So. That's that. Don't try that again, please. It goes against the agreement.

I'll bet you the needles haven't deflected even a bit. Not so much as a twitch. Very primitive instruments those, but what else do the surgeons have to rely on. The optic nerve, which, unfortunately, lies in the immediate proximity of the operative field, is under constant observation, or so they claim. No comment. Or are we perhaps to imagine the optic nerve being as thick as the thread used at home to sew on buttons. No, they said, you told me, the optic nerve was in no acute danger. Not another word about the optic nerve, not so much as a thought. How am I supposed to know with which sense, or senses, you may be taking in everything I am imagining ever so furtively. Seeing hearing smelling tasting touching—and that's all there is? Who believes that, anyway. We can't have been sent on our way with so little sensitivity back then. Although the demand for a built-in Geiger counter does sound rather pretentious, even humorous. Who could have predicted all those millions of years ago that it would one day enhance our species' chances of survival,

   although, on the other hand, I wasn't really dying to know how the lush green meadow in front of the house would have registered on a Geiger counter today. However, I did decide to throw away those few dandelion leaves, the smallest and most tender, that I had automatically picked in passing, as I did every other day, for my noonday salad. That is also what both the small and large radios, which were tuned to different stations, again advised unanimously on the hour: no greens. No fresh milk for the children. A new name for danger is being circulated: Iodine 131. It turns out that the thyroid is one of our most sensitive organs for storing radioactive iodine. The stock of iodine tablets in the pharmacies in the vicinity of one of the stations has been bought up since yesterday by those people who foresee even improbable developments. This, I have been informed, was neither necessary nor advisable. Normal iodine did indeed shield the thyroid from the other, harmful one, but . . .

At which point I had to make a quick call to Berlin, but they had already heard. Greens and spinach weren't available anyway, and she was no longer giving the children fresh milk, said my youngest daughter. (O *milk of inhuman kindness, bitter potion* . . .) Although she had been in the sandbox with them yesterday afternoon and had, unfortunately, bathed them afterwards. What, hadn't I heard? One was supposed to shower the children after they had been outside. Bathing relaxed the skin, opening the pores and washing the radioactivity into the body with a vengeance. Exaggerated? If only one knew.

I asked about her voice. Why it sounded as it did. It sounded as you'd expect a voice to sound if one wasn't sleeping at night, she said. And of course I would want to know why she wasn't sleeping at night and so she would rather tell me right away of her own accord that word had only just reached her now that it was too late, and there were the children lying in their beds and she just couldn't bear the sight and so she just couldn't sleep, and now could I name her a better reason for insomnia.

Yes, I said. No. On the other hand . . .

Mother! she broke in, I should just stop right there. As if I didn't know better. They'll never ever learn, said my youngest daughter. They're all sick. Or what more would have to happen apart from pouring away thousands of liters of milk and having to live in fear of poisoning the children especially quickly with especially healthful foods. While the children on the other side of the earth were perishing for lack of those very foods.

During a lull in our conversation, it once again seemed to me that our thoughts were chafing on a cunningly well-hidden secret. I also saw a sequence of pictures which I don't intend to describe. Yet I wondered whether I shouldn't have long since described in harsher and more ruthless (against myself!) terms those very pictures which I saw before me, knowing all the while that was not the question. And although I sensed that everything going on inside me remained blurred, inadequate in every sense of the word, I was once more forced to admire the way in which everything fits together with a sleepwalker's precision: the desire of most people for a comfortable life, their tendency to believe the speakers on raised platforms and the men in white coats; the addiction to harmony and the fear of contradiction of the many seem to correspond to the arrogance and hunger for power, the dedication to profit, unscrupulous inquisitiveness, and self-infatuation of the few. So what was it that didn't add up in this equation?

I asked my daughter to tell me something else, preferably about the children. Whereupon I heard that the little one had pranced about the kitchen, a wing nut on his thumb, his hand held high: Me Punch. Me Punch. I was thrilled by the image. How did he know about Punch and Judy, anyway. And was it normal for a child of one and a half to turn himself into someone else. Not only himself, she said, but every possible object. A whisk with a potholder on its head was an old woman who danced on the kitchen table, and when Marie gave her a smack with another potholder and the old biddy started griping, the little one cried so hard the big tears just flowed down his cheeks and they had to stop playing.

Little boys, I said. All they have to put them through to toughen them up.

They got their revenge later, said my youngest daughter, she was sure of it. Whoever had the ability to love beaten out of him would surely prevent others from loving in turn.

We would have to make sure it didn't happen to the little one, I said.

Over my dead body, said my youngest daughter, and told me about Marie. Marie had a friend, Julius. She would bring him home from nursery school almost every day, and they would sit down, away from the others, hand in hand on a little bench and ask one another: Are you my friend? I am your friend. Are you my friend, too? And then they would eat from the same piece of cake and drink from one cup, and the little one would plant himself solidly before them, hands behind his back, listening to them and watching them greedily and devoutly.

You know what, I said, Shakespeare and Greek tragedy wouldn't do a thing for me now compared with your children's stories. And, by the way, did she know that the radiation level at the time of the above-ground nuclear-weapons tests in the 1960s was said to have been higher than now.

You sure know how to make a person feel good, said my youngest daughter . . .

The house and the meadow toward the street side were completely bathed in sunshine now. One could see that this was going to be one of the most beautiful days of the year. You're missing it, brother. Whatever sensations might be occupying your senses, this day is not one of them. This immaculate blue sky, this incarnation of purity, where the uneasy glances of millions are meeting today, is lost to you. After the clean, hook-shaped incision above your right eyebrow, after all the blood vessels have been meticulously clamped, the scalp stretched apart as far as possible to both sides, the brain pushed aside and wrapped in foil, your doctors are presumably concentrating on getting as close to the root of evil as possible without damaging the pituitary gland. Namely because, as the young nurse informed you, even personality changes can result from damage to certain parts of the brain. Nice prospects, you said, and I asked bluntly if you were really that attached to your personality. I've grown accustomed to it, you said. A patient who had formerly been peaceful suddenly became aggressive and attacked the nurses. You see, you said, that could be another solution to the peace problem: implanting an electrode into every newborn baby. Yes, I countered, brave new world.

Incidentally, the frontal lobes are not merely responsible for your deliberate behavior; they also contain most of the centers of association. In the case of humans, consciousness. I had to picture very precise and careful instruments—was metal even remotely feasible?—which could be suitable to probe into the region where your consciousness dwells . . .

Our soil is definitely too heavy for growing vegetables. Loamy soil, hard, hard as a rock after three rainless days, nearly impossible to till. Still I tried to break up the soil with a hoe and a rake to lay out beds in which I could trace furrows with a stick, not too deep and not too shallow, into which to spread the round brown sorrel seeds for sorrel soup, the minute, pointy lettuce seeds and the spinach seeds, all this very thoroughly and angrily, which I noticed only because I had been accompanying my activities with half-audible curses until I stopped and asked myself just as audibly: What for?

Because now they've even killed our appetite for lettuce and spinach.

Who, they.

The remaining bed under the apple tree will be planted with garden cress. It "requires tender loving care in order to safeguard the survival of vitamins A, C, D, and E and iodine." All of a sudden I found myself wondering whether the perpetrators of those kinds of technology whose hellish danger is part and parcel of their very essence have ever in their lives put into the soil kernels so minute that they stick to the fingertips, later to see them sprout and to watch the plants' growth for weeks, for months. I immediately recognized my fallacy, since everybody has heard or read that hardworking scientists and technicians are just the ones who frequently seek relaxation through gardening. Or does this thesis apply only to the older ones; is it outdated with regard to the younger generation, those who now have the final say? I resolved to make a list of those activities and pleasures which, more than likely, are foreign to those men of science and technology. To what end? In all honesty: I don't know. I was simply wondering whether the various compartments of our brain didn't perhaps interact with one another in such a way that a woman who has been nursing her infant for months would be prohibited by a blockage in a certain part of her brain from supporting with word and deed those new technologies which can poison her milk.

I circle the house. I've opened all the windows wide, not only to let in the heat but also to be sure of hearing the telephone. At least the currant bushes and the cherry trees, newly planted this year, have taken root. The grass seed has sprouted; our wish for a thick, expansive lawn is going to come true. The mallow plants on the side of the house have shot up and there are even two dahlias breaking through the earth's crust with the tips of their delicate leaves. That's it, I heard myself say. That's the stuff. It's not your fault. You're doing your part.

The radiant sky. Now one can't think that anymore,

either. We can do without radiation treatment in view of the histological findings, your doctor will tell you, but we haven't come to that point yet. At the moment we've only reached the point of urgently wishing for such a fortunate course of events.

It was still much too early for the call I had been expecting and yet I ran into the house when the phone rang. I recognized the woman's voice, although we do not speak often on the phone. She only wanted to hear my voice. That was a good idea of hers. Whether I actually knew that she liked me. I had hoped as much. And assumed as much. Now I knew. Yes. And it made me happy. It was just one of those days. "Chain reaction" was a phrase which had already scared her to death as a child. I was no longer a child when the phrase came into usage. By the way, they were operating on my brother today. Oh. She hadn't even known that I had a brother. Anything serious? Then she wouldn't tie up the line any longer.

I saw her, thin, hunched, her movements economical within her room, succumbing to the ever advancing clutter of books and manuscripts. The bizarre lines which thoughts and words might describe in her mind ere they, still bizarre yet each precisely in its place, go down on paper. Her old desk. Her rear window overlooking a Berlin courtyard. I reflected on how friendliness simplifies the understanding of another person for me, which was sometimes difficult with this friend. Perhaps, she had added, she should just try harder to make herself understood. Wasn't unintelligibility also a kind of defense mechanism? At which point I warned of the consequences of such confessions for the evaluation of entire bodies of literature.

Sentiment is not called for, least of all today.

The glaze is off the planet, don't you think? said the friend. The sentence shoved its way to the front of the papers on my desk as I tentatively approached, mindful of those enviable fellow members of the guild who, fanatics of the word all—surrounded by myriad forms of death, destruction, perdition, and threat—steadfastly followed the line begun at one point in their writing toward a goal, without ever drawing any closer. I sat down on my swivel chair, looking through the pages, reading individual sentences, and found that they left me cold. They, or I myself, or both of us had changed and I was reminded of certain documents where the true, the secret writing appears only after chemical treatment, whereby the original, deliberately irrelevant text is revealed to be a pretext. I saw the writing on my pages fade and possibly disappear under the effect of radiation and it was still uncertain whether a permanent subtext would ever appear between the lines. I was having a new experience with a wicked kind of freedom. I saw that there also exists the freedom to refuse to obey anything, even self-imposed duties. For the first time I faced the possibility that even duties such as these can disintegrate and I realized that no habit would be strong enough to take their place. Ah. How joyously would I move toward a goal, without ever drawing any closer.

But how could I move without a goal?

Relieved, if that's the proper word here, I gave myself some time off. No words today. I stayed seated for a while, staring at the lawn and the elderberry hedge behind the house, which was not nearly as full as it would be in three or four weeks. Then I got up, went out, and began to wreak havoc among the weeds with my bare hands. First I pulled up the grass around the small, newly planted bushes that were suffocating. A tiny forsythia was preparing to blossom. Absurd, I said, clearing a space for it. My thoughts turned once again to my friend and I found myself wondering why I sometimes have to shield myself against her, whenever I have occasion to believe that she has drawn away from me. Loss of empathy is always, or nearly always, a prelude to the fall, not merely into uncertainty, but also into hostility. Yet how is it that antipathy and apathy have the power to make us resemble the image they have of us. In the shade the grass was still wet with dew. I was going at it like a machine, all the while trying to erase my thoughts as a machine does its program. I warned the frenchweed which was advancing toward us from the edge of the meadow: Your time will come, just you wait. Although I know from past experience that one can never get rid of frenchweed once it has taken root. At the stroke of the hour I heard on my little radio that one would be well advised to wear gloves today if working in the garden was unavoidable, and I heard a sound escape my throat which resembled a manic clarion call of triumph, while fervently continuing to pull weeds with my bare hands. Well, we'll see about that, I retorted . . .

Of course I don't know whether they were already using cat or sheep gut in your head at that point, brother, a type of suture which later dissolves by itself, but I doubt it very much. It was as yet too early for that. They were still preoccupied with maintaining the connection between the pituitary gland and the brain, or some such thing—which, if I may get ahead of myself, was successful—while nonetheless forging radically ahead. This, in a case like yours, can only mean peeling out from its healthy environment the tumor which was nestled very, very snugly up against the pituitary gland—root and branch, indeed down to the last cell. And being aware each second that every square millimeter of this environment is highly sensitive. That damaging it can cause those dreaded "mishaps" whose victims you could observe in other hospital rooms and which we shied away from discussing openly. Rather than getting caught up in all that, I turned my attention to the nettles,

this time, however, wearing my pink rubber gloves. It is indescribably satisfying to grab hold of a nettle bush with one's right hand while digging along the length of its root with the index finger of the left hand until the right spot has been found, from which the entire length of the tough, deep, branched rootstock can be pulled out, gingerly and steadily. That's that. You won't be doing any more damage. Simultaneously, wordlessly, at a deeper level of my consciousness, I assured the Lord of the Nettles, or whatever spirit of nature is responsible for more all-encompassing contexts, that I was not intending to wage war against all nettles; that I was well aware that five species of butterfly depended on nettles for nourishment. And that these butterflies would still make a decent living here. However, that plant whose name I don't even know, a sticky, single-minded weed anchored in the earth by a single, threadlike root whose appearance belies its strength, is something different altogether. The little leaves which it brings forth could be mistaken for needles. After making its first appearance last year in the clearing between the elderberry bushes, it seems to want to take over the entire back lawn this year, especially the freshly dug-up mound where the newly seeded grass has hardly begun to sprout, compared with masses of that damned weed. Just you wait! I said out loud. Just you wait! That was the way my maternal grandfather used to talk. To the devil with you! I wonder how my grandfather pictured the devil. You, I say to the weeds, I'm going to wipe you out! That's a promise. Regardless of the survival of the species.

I was in Kiev only once in my life, in May it was. I remember white houses. Sloping streets. Lots of green, blossoms. The monument to the dead of World War II on the hill above the Dnieper. Hazy images

lost amid similar remembrances of other cities. Hazy
as well the memory of a love which must have been
fresh back then. Someday, soon, everything will have
become memory for me. Someday, perhaps already
in three, in four weeks—may the time pass quickly—
the memory of this day will have gone out of focus
as well. Unforgettable: looking out over the Dniepcr,
mighty Eastern river. The bend of the river. The plain
beyond. And the sky. A sky such as this, pure blue.

". . . *Aghast, the mothers search the sky for the
inventions of learned men . . ."* Now we have reached
that point. But they can search for a long time, they
won't see anything. It is only the suspicion gnawing
within them that colors the innocent sky such a poi-
sonous shade. The malignant sky. So the mothers sit
down by the radio and attempt to learn the new
words. Becquerel. Explanations—by scientists who,
unimpeded by any sense of awe as to what holds
nature together there at its innermost core, wish not
only to know but also to implement. Half-life is what
the mothers learn today. Iodine 131. Cesium. Explanations by other scientists who contradict what the
first ones said; who are furious and helpless. Now all
of that was drizzling down upon us together with the
carriers of radioactive substances, such as rain,

but you, brother, and may the steady hand of your
surgeon preserve your eyesight, will no more get to
see it than we will. Calling it "cloud" is merely an
indication of our inability to keep pace linguistically
with the progress of science. Incessantly gathering in-

formation and comparing the new with the previously recorded, our perception apparatus—whose headquarters, I have been told, along with those of the language center, are in the left hemisphere of the brain, where the advanced cognitive functions of the human convene—usually selects that name to designate a new phenomenon which shows the highest number of shared characteristics with those material manifestations which it has known since time immemorial. That's how you would explain the process to me. That is approximately how you explained it to me only recently, when you demonstrated the program stored in your personal computer. I saw how you relished its obedience when you called up the program. You see. It understood. Now it's searching for PH 1. Do you see that? READY. So now I press this key. Now it's calculating for us how an arbitrary emission spreads out from its source when that source is twenty meters above the earth's surface. So, let's take a chimney. And the emission can be, for instance, sulfurous smoke. There. And so that you can take it all in at one glance: blipblipblipblipblip: the corresponding graph. That is the advantage of this system, it also does diagrams. Now you can see the curve: quite a sharp rise up to about two hundred meters and then, here, the peak: at a given chimney height of twenty meters, the maximum concentration of pollution would be expected to lie along a circle with a radius of approximately two hundred meters from the source of emission. And, of course, the higher the chimney, the farther the imission area from the source. What shall we say. How about a chimney thirty meters high. The key. READY. Blipblipblipblip: the figures. Now the graph key again. There you go. The peak has moved noticeably. Which was to be expected. So, dear brother, if you had your computer by your bedside you could calculate the drift of our cloud—provided you had the initial data, such as divergence, height of the reactor, wind velocity, to feed into your computer. But you don't . . .

How strange that *a-tom* in Greek means the same as *in-dividuum* in Latin: unsplittable. The inventors of these words knew neither nuclear fission nor schizophrenia. Whence the modern compulsion to split into ever smaller parts, to split off entire parts of the personality from that ancient being once thought indivisible . . .

I wonder whether the brain, the only human organ which—apart from heart and lungs—remains active even during sleep, actually takes a rest under deepest anesthesia. Whether it can at least stop for a few hours in its restless search for impulses and stop drawing upon substitute sources should its environment fail to provide genuine impulses. Squandering its immense surplus energy on substitute problems: unfathomable, and thus the wrong way to approach the question. No surgeon could penetrate through to that hectic group of neural connections in the brains of those men who thought up the procedures for the so-called peaceful utilization of nuclear energy. Whose constant agitation was to be pacified only by working on precisely those problems which the untamed atom posed its tamers. I hazard the hypothesis that they wouldn't have known what to do with themselves save for this goal; they would have had to suffer immeasurably under their overdeveloped cerebral activity . . .

You'll think this unfair of me, brother, and I am reluctant to be, or to appear to be, unfair, you know that; but do you know why? Because I attempt to deflect and divert the hurtful injustices of others by means of justice against all. So I will grant you—later; not today; no, not today—that those men in pursuit of the peaceful atom were being spurred on by a utopia: enough energy for all and for all time. Could they have known otherwise in time? When was I first confronted by their adversaries? Let me think. It was at the beginning of the seventies, the name of the power plant was Wyhl, it didn't get built. The young people who pressed upon us the first material about the dangers of the "peaceful" utilization of nuclear energy were ridiculed, rebuked, reprimanded. Among others, by scientists who were defending their work and, I hope, their utopia. "Monsters"? But did I say they were monsters? Do the utopias of our time necessarily breed monsters? Were we monsters when we, for the sake of a utopia we were not willing to postpone— justice, equality, humanity for all—fought those in whose interest this utopia was not (is not), and, with our own doubts, fought those who dared doubt that the ends justify the means? That science, the new god,

held all the answers we would seek from him? Is this
the wrong approach to the question? Have I only too
gladly seized upon the pretext provided by this day
to take time off from my manuscript, mired in false
questions, tentative approaches, and inadequate,
therefore countless, beginnings, since I have been
moving in futile circles around this question, wrongly
posed more likely than not, for days, weeks? One
seeks out the point of greatest pain and simultaneously flees; I should know, brother, whence this sensation of being torn apart comes; understand—my
God, yes, of course I can understand trying to escape
that feeling, all the way out into the cosmos or, for
that matter, right into the atom . . .

A list of the activities which these men of science
and technology presumably do not pursue or which,
if forced upon them, they would consider a waste of
time: Changing a baby's diapers. Cooking, shopping
with a child on one's arm or in the baby carriage.
Doing the laundry, hanging it up to dry, taking it
down, folding it, ironing it, darning it. Sweeping the
floor, mopping it, polishing it, vacuuming it. Dusting.
Sewing. Knitting. Crocheting. Embroidering. Doing
the dishes. Doing the dishes. Doing the dishes. Taking
care of a sick child. Thinking up stories to tell. Singing
songs. And how many of these activities do I myself
consider a waste of time?

I have read: Humans, incomplete and imperfect,
could also be defined as beings actively in search of
their optimal development. I—that I which tends to

split off from "me" for purposes of contemplation—
I was a funny sight standing in the clearing amid the
elderberry bushes, taking in again and again the view
across the green field of grain, descending in great
waves to the sea, a picture which I could become
addicted to, and asking myself: What do people want?
I guess, dear brother: people want to experience
strong emotions and they want to be loved. Period.
Deep down, everybody knows that, and if the gratification of their deepest desires is not granted, does
not succeed, or is denied, then they—no, we!—create
substitute gratification and cling to a substitute life,
a substitute for life, the entire breathlessly expanding
monstrous technological creation, a substitute for
love. Everything they call progress and which I cling
to as well, brother heart, whether I want to or
not, nothing but devices to trigger strong emotions
(" . . . With my thighs wrapped around those racing
engines, I am so infinitely greater than my wimp of a
boss . . .")—can one say that; are we the last generation to believe that strong emotions may be triggered in us only by other people, everything else is
blasphemous, depraved,

but now the telephone has just started ringing again
and I run as fast as I can into the house through the
back door, through the corridor still cold from winter,
the dark entrance hall into the big parlor where the
bright red telephone, God bless it, sits on the wooden
chest, where, once I finally had the receiver in my
hand, the voice of your wife, my sister-in-law, in-

formed me there was still no news about you. They were still operating, the nurse had told her. You couldn't be back on the ward before 2 p.m. A very long time, we both thought, six hours, that was a long time indeed, and we didn't dare ask one another what to make of such a lengthy operation; in fact, we said only the basics, for we were both afraid that one word too many might burst the dam, which still had to hold.

So I went back outside through the front porch and on my way decided to make a quick inspection of the flowerpots on the windowsills and was pleasantly shocked: the zucchini plants had sprouted! Seventeen seedlings in eight pots. I took each one in my hand and examined the pale green, furled little leaves, each and every one, poking through the soil with their elbows, so to speak, namely stem first, only later in the following days to stand up and unfurl their leaves, with seeds like pumpkin seeds, from which they had grown, sticking to their tips—a process I do not understand; which, I believe, no one really understands. Why did it mean so much to me that the zucchini had sprouted. I envisaged the plants in the sun bed having grown larger, first sprouting their seed leaves during fair weather, then pushing out their rough stems, snakelike, in unbridled growth, to become entangled with those of the other plants. Saw the large blossoms, glowing yellow. Their fruits, cucumberlike, beautifully shaped, glistening dark green. Meals outdoors, the high point of which will be the breaded zucchini fritters, basted with garlic sauce. Yes. Summer would come again. All of us together, many people, we would sit around the huge table made once again from two wooden horses and the light green door, on which I would spread the oilcloth with the blue flowers, weighted down against the wind with stones in all four corners. I had to go to the stable right then, immediately, to check whether the door and the wooden horses were still there, nothing was more important to me at that moment. In the old chicken coop, I found a bag of peaty soil which would come in handy, but not the door. In the old stable, everything was neatly stacked and leaned up against the wall: door, wooden horses, and the bicycles in front. The bicycles! I pulled one out, had only to pump up the front tire and pushed it out the door. There was just enough time to ride to the co-op before it closed.

A Red Cross ambulance stood in the deserted village street and I assumed that one of the lonely old women in the former farmworkers' dwellings had fallen ill and was being taken to the hospital. But there was no one there whom I could have asked. It wasn't the mother of the co-op branch manager, in any case, although she had not left her bed for weeks and had to be cared for by her daughter. If anything had happened to her, the second salesgirl would have known. I counted out the bottles of milk I had ordered as I put them into my bag, and asked whether everybody was picking up their milk today as usual. Sure, the salesgirl said, they were all buying their milk same as

always, what else could they do? It was terrible, just
terrible, she said, the likes of us couldn't do anything
about it anyhow. After all, one couldn't stop eating
and drinking. Young Prochnow, who works in the
cowshed, came in for a couple of bottles of beer and
gave me a knowing look. I understood what he was
trying to say. This past fall, sitting at our kitchen table,
he had voiced his firm conviction that there existed
extraterrestrial beings, spirits, who were far ahead of
us in every respect and had our earth firmly under
their control. Who were allowing human madness free
reign but would step in, at the very last second, when
we were poised on the brink of self-destruction. Of
course Fritz Prochnow didn't know how either, but
they would—of that he was absolutely certain. Now,
in the co-op, he said to me: You see. We don't even
need a war. We manage to blow ourselves up in times
of peace. So? I said. You wait! young Prochnow said.
He reads all the books on astronomy and futurology
and every utopian novel he can lay his hands on. No
one can tell him that the human race was created and
condemned to shoulder all the drudgery of its development, to suffer all that it must, only to exterminate
itself in the end. No one can tell me that, he said. Let
those without children believe that. I have three children. I don't believe that.

Keeping a firm grip on the handlebars, I rode back
on the sloping cobblestone street beneath the old lime
trees, past the ancient village church, no longer in use.
The Red Cross ambulance was gone and I wondered

whether Fritz Prochnow's way of seeing things—that we are all remote-controlled beings whose strings are jerked by the hands of others—made it any easier on him, or not. A few old women had congregated on the street and I paused briefly to hear that it was Herr Weiss who had been taken away by the Red Cross ambulance: he had fallen down, no longer in control of his senses, it didn't look good for him. My bicycle took the curve to the row of post-office boxes with a will all its own; half a dozen letters spilled out when the metal flap fell open. I had to tug at the newspapers. I glanced at the return addresses on the letters as I pushed my bicycle down the street. Two or three piqued my curiosity . . .

It remains an unpleasant notion that a skullbone, a frontal bone for example, is handled no differently than a piece of metal, technically speaking, when one wishes to cut out a segment. One uses a drill. And a simple mechanical pump is presumably used to pump out the cerebral fluid which would otherwise hinder the actual operation. Partially responsible for the inevitable headache following the operation is the lack of cerebral fluid, which is only gradually restored . . .

Once again, so it seemed, our age had created a Before and After for itself. I realized that I could describe my life as a series of just such incisions, a gradual clouding over produced by ever thickening shadows. Or, on the contrary, as a continuous acclimatization to ever harsher lighting, sharper insights, increasing matter-of-factness. Although I knew that my choice of the path over the grassy knoll was not entirely coincidental, nor entirely without motive my gaze across the wide patch of clover where our searches have often been rewarded with a four-leaf clover, I nonetheless gave a shout of joy at the sight of a large specimen. I find them only when no one is there to find them for me.

Marvellous Nature Shining on Me!

Perhaps the problem of what to do with the libraries full of nature poems is not the most urgent. But it is a problem all the same, I thought. I realized that I was standing on the exact spot which I had sought to avoid over the last week, unless I had a craving for four-leaf clovers. Ever since that family—father, mother, son; and the mother grew up in this very same house where we now spend our summers—walked across the meadow last week and looked around, as people tend to look around, when they know what they're looking for. Ever since that woman, today a nurse, portly and permed, held forth on what happened here in the summer of '45 on the very spot where I stood. If she would only stop harping on it! the tall, lanky son interrupted, but the woman didn't see why she shouldn't tell her story: Here, precisely here, her father had been picked up by the Russians back then. In a military vehicle, Karsten! And her father had stroked her little brother's hair and said: Don't cry, I'll be back soon, this is just a mistake. But come back he did not. Why not? What had he done? Nothing, that was just it. He had done nothing, he was a driver—a driver for the Gestapo, said the boy, who, bored as he was, had been contemplating the barn, and left after pronouncing this second sentence. Then the husband butted in sharply: A driver, yes! and that was surely no reason, for God's sake! He set off after the boy. The wife still had to recount how her mother, who had then leased the land, had worked her fingers to the bone all those years for her four children. And how she had always sat up there in front of the porch when the children were grown up and came to visit, and waved goodbye when they drove off again. Just as I stand there now and wave when visitors drive off. Just as our neighbor Heinrich Plaack is sitting there now in his typical bent-over posture, elbows propped on his knees, breathing heavily, something I noticed only upon drawing nearer. He just wanted the key to the garage to get him some seed potatoes. Just see if we don't get a few potatoes into the ground today. Weather's obliging. If only it just didn't start raining again.

No, I said, that we could do without. The lifetime of Heinrich Plaack spans seventy years of trouble and toil, and how exquisite that it has not taught him to say anything other than what he really thinks. He thinks we have had enough rain this year for the time being, the soil is saturated and can nourish the potatoes and other seeds for a long time. As I agree with him, I think of the cloud and how it wanders about more and more threateningly in search of a weather situation which allows it to rain itself out. How even regions which normally beg for rain are now dying to miss out. Let the others get soaked. We have umbrella, raincoat, and rubber boots at the ready in case of emergency. Should it rain tomorrow, or the day after, we won't let our children go to school, not even as far as the bus stop. We shall also forbid them to sing: It's raining / It's pouring / The old man is snoring. Alongside the one God who created and rules over the earth there exists, in the opinion of some deviationists, another God, who did not create and does not rule over the earth. A foreign, unknown God. By concentrating my every thought and wish upon him, it did come to pass that I realized him. An instance's sensation which no one dare expect me to put into words. Only this: If I remember correctly, the eyesight, that focal point of our perceptive powers, was hardly involved in my sensation, if at all. And yet I sensed that a supreme, possibly self-destructive effort on my part could coax the power or force or energy or potency which suddenly surrounded me (an atmosphere condensed to the point of pain) into materializing: into showing its face. I didn't dare make this effort. Hurriedly, hurriedly did I ease the tension, just before it became unbearable, and my fear was great. A fear tinged with disappointment. I gave up, that much is undeniable. It was not him that I feared, the Antigod. I feared the depths in myself—that is to say: beneath my skullcap—out of which such an unbeing might rise . . .

We are not conditioned, brother, to weather those electrical storms which burst uncontrollably from time to time in our brains and to risk letting them have their way with us. Certain reaction patterns are wired together in our brains—that is the expression used by biologists, heedless of the unpleasant picture such words suggest. It is understandable that one and the same reaction wending its way through the jungle of the brain anew each time in response to one and the same impulse would be too ineffective, much too time-consuming: a being with such a nervous system would have had little chance of survival. But it is certainly not wires that the surgeons are finding (they will, however, leave some metal behind: gold clamps used to clamp the bleeding vessels); they are finding that mass which would dissolve into cells beneath the microscope: neurons; and they could, with strong magnification, find those connectors between the neurons called "synapses," which number greater than the total amount of primary particles in the universe. This, brother heart, is one of the few figures which can get me excited. Might not the evolutionary exuberance in the case of our brain, of all things, however many hundreds of thousands of years it may have taken, have been too much of a good thing . . .

I suddenly realized that old Plaack had been talking to me for some time about his brother-in-law, the man who had been a driver for the Gestapo and had died in a Soviet camp quite nearby in 1945. So old Plaack must have heard that his niece had told me about it.

A Day's News

I have, on more than one occasion, noticed that the time he needs before talking about difficult things is longer than the time I need. And that the store of themes about which he would never speak must be greater than my own. My brother-in-law, he said to me, was never aware of anything bad. If he had of been aware of something, he sure would have cleared out.

He may be right about that. I saw before me those same automobiles which, without drivers, never could have driven, transported, taken, delivered anyone anywhere. That's just the point, I felt like saying, but didn't. We remained silent for a time. Then Heinrich Plaack said: Now they're even getting the clouds all mixed up . . .

Just to give you the most important news, which you're missing in your sleep, or half sleep: Last Saturday, at 1:25 local time, there was a fire in the tower house of the fourth reactor block. Several unhappy circumstances of an unforeseeable nature had to occur simultaneously to set it off. That which might have happened once in ten thousand years at most, according to the physicists, has now happened. Ten thousand years have melted down to this one day. The law of averages has made clear to us that it wishes to be taken seriously. The physicists continue talking to us in their incomprehensible language. What are "fifteen millirems of fallout per hour"? How long would I, how long would a child of one, how long would an embryo in the womb have to be exposed to it in order to be harmed. Now we hear that every new technology requires sacrifices at first. I tried to steel myself against the faces of people which might appear—did appear—on television, who would try to force a smile. Whose hair would have fallen out. Whose doctors would use the word "brave." A graphite fire which no one could have expected, as we shall be told, is, however, extraordinarily hard to put out once it has started. But someone had to do it. Talk was of two casualties on that day of which I am still speaking so that it won't be completely lost to you. That whole day I couldn't get a certain expression out of my head: the glowing core. Now that person two thousand kilometers away is smothering the glowing core of our forbidden desires with concrete, sand, and lead. The word "catastrophe" is not permitted as long as there is danger of catastrophe turning to doom. You, I assume, are familiar with all the possible interpretations of the technical term "China syndrome" . . .

I had missed the transition once again; old Plaack's story had progressed. Had I ever noticed that he had only one eye? Now I secretly admired how closely the color of a glass eye can match that of a real one. The loss of an eye had saved his life. Sometimes life went all haywire. When things started getting heavy, ultimately, on the Russian front, he had taken out his glass eye, stuck it in his pocket, and put a bandage over the empty socket, thus appearing so wounded that every task force had sent him farther behind the front, and the dirtier his bandage became, the better off he was. And if thy right eye offend thee . . .

Heinrich Plaack was the first man I met who still suffered when he told me about the war, about "our boys." No person could tell the worst things of all, he said. But just a small example: In France, where the people had all fled before us, the houses stood empty, bag and baggage packed. They had to leave everything behind. And so, with his gear all dirty and ragged, he had also gone into a house once and taken a fresh shirt his size and a pair of socks, he was the first to admit it. But he had still taken care not to disturb anything else, to leave everything in order. When he had come by again the next day, however, it looked as if the place had been a stopover for vandals. His own brothers-in-arms had had a go at the trunks and suitcases. They had broken everything open, they had pulled the fresh, clean bed linen onto the floor and then they had stomped around on it, for nothing and no good reason, just feeling boisterous and looking for kicks. Then he had said to his lieutenant, who was an all right guy when you got him alone: Things ain't going right, sir, he had said, and the lieutenant had replied: Right you are, Heinrich. No respect for anything—there was no way things could go right . . .

I don't want to be pushy. But it's slowly getting toward noon and the likes of us can't really imagine what a good team of trained specialists could be up

to for so many hours with—or more correctly: in—
your head, brother. I will admit, the fact that these
people, like all specialists, cannot share the holy terror
of the yawning abyss of their particular field with us
lay people is a bit disconcerting; in other words, they
have lost, through unavoidable professional routine,
your and my reverend fear of operating within that
sphere in which is decided whether we are one way
or another; whether we still recognize ourselves after
the operation is over. What amount, what kind of
"mishaps," "defects" we can accept, tolerate, if need
be, without becoming strangers to ourselves. If one
of the senses must be sacrificed, then, as anyone would
say, let it be the sense of smell. But I was able to save
your sense of taste, your doctor will say to you, and
you won't know whether he was forced to decide
for you and in your place at a moment's notice between smell and sight. The sense of taste? Not completely. Certain types of beer will taste a bit like soap
from now on . . . Beer one can do without, brother.

Beer and what else? By the way, the senses of smell
and taste are supposedly "often coupled" in the lower
animals. The first mammals presumably developed
around two hundred million years ago from mammal-
like reptiles which succumbed to the other reptiles in
the battle over ecological niches and took over the
relatively empty nocturnal niches—a way of existence
crucially dependent on hearing and smell, senses of
distance which were thus treated to preferential development. A few branches of the vertebrate family

tree led to dead ends. It remains to be seen whether that branch which resulted in the human being will also lead to a dead end. *Man in the Holocene.* If one were to transpose the data of the development of life on earth onto a scale of twenty-four hours, the vertebrates would begin to evolve at around 9:30 p.m., the first hominids around 11:57 p.m. At three seconds to midnight, brother, humankind enters the world stage. Intelligence becomes the decisive evolutionary factor. Intelligent humanity creates the means of subjugating nature and its own kind. It seeks to break the rules and norms which it has imposed upon itself by means of open or concealed aggression, even at the cost of self-annihilation,

so that, I must add here, although this footnote might seem a bit trivial, a man like Heinrich Plaack, former farm hand, then farmer in a cooperative society, now retired, sits on the stone balustrade in front of the former parish house at the end of his life, elbows resting on his knees, hands hanging down between his knees, head lowered, and has to ask himself: What is the matter here. What is the matter with some people. It was really as if some people had a worm in their heads that wouldn't let them alone, he said. They'd had one like that in their company, he still had to think of him. Such a big shot. Such a good-for-nothing. Do you know what kind of rottenness the guy was capable of?

I couldn't persuade old Plaack to keep his story to himself, although I could sense right down to the roots of my hair that he was just about to add a further exhibit to my inner gallery of unforgettable horrors: the story of the young Russian soldier who emerges from the swamps, exhausted and almost frozen, days after the other members of his unit, and that vile fellow from Heinrich Plaack's company forces him to take off his boots, after which he must run to the POW camp behind the lines. At forty below zero, Heinrich Plaack said, can you believe that. Listen, I said, think of what you're doing, he'll never make it! But he only tossed his head, the rotten bum. And the boots didn't even fit him. You'll be sorry someday, I said to him. Your day will come. And a few weeks later when he lay there screaming with a bullet in his belly, I told him: You just be quiet. You just think of the Russian, what you did to him. Then his eyes just rolled back and he didn't make another sound—and thus I shall always see the look on the face of the young Russian, the young German tossing his head, and then the way he lay there, his eyes rolling back. Nope, said old Plaack, you can never forget that. Never. Whoever says so is lying.

The telephone. I started running. That same friend again. Was there any word of my brother. Don't know yet, I said, they're still operating. Aha. Then once again she wouldn't tie up the line any longer.

Sometimes, brother, you get caught up in such diffuse circumstances that you don't even know what you should actually be thinking about. Physiologically speaking, that must be represented by a flickering in several parts of the brain, I would assume. A precautionary allocation of as yet nondirectional energy which does not flow unswervingly into the prepaved compound network, but rather gropes about in unexplored territory before gathering itself, for example, into a question: Whence this desire for fission, for fire and explosions!

You forbade me to use the word "desire" in this connection. Desire, desire . . . you said. That was another one of those exaggerated, partisan expressions. It was much simpler than that. Once someone had begun to invent something. Or to discover something. Or to develop something: then he just couldn't stop anymore. Whoever was on the trail of the fissionable atom, for example, couldn't just cancel his experiments. Like the rats, I said, continuously pressing the "desire button." But that was just my question. Where is the center of desire in the brains of those scientists?

I would never entirely understand the titillation which had seduced that handful of most highly gifted physicists and chemists into forging ahead half a century ago, in another age, I said. "The others" would do it if they didn't—such a weak argument. From today's perspective! you said. You're not taking into account the time they needed just to comprehend what they had discovered there. You honestly don't think they sat down together and decided: Now let's discover uranium fission! Or even: the atom bomb! They decided that later on, I said. Later on was war, you answered. Indeed! I said, and you said I shouldn't be so presumptuous. I should rather think of myself. Whether I would be able to stop. Whether I hadn't once told him that words could wound, even destroy, like projectiles; whether I was always able to judge— always willing to judge—when my words would wound, perhaps destroy? At what level of destruction I would back down? No longer say what I could? Opt for silence?

That was the turning point of the day.

After a certain time, which remains a blank in my mind, I found myself in the kitchen, foolishly stacking dirty dishes in the cupboard. All at once I observed myself weighing in my hand like a projectile one of the ceramic cups out of which we like to drink tea. And then put it back on its shelf, firmly, but without breaking it, reached for the olivewood salad utensils and, with a precise and accurately aimed throw, whipped them into the corner. Picked them up, threw them into the corner again with all my might. And again. And again. Take that. And that. And that. I'll show you. I'm so fed up with you. Fed up. Fed up.

I observed myself with satisfaction. The rage, the hate in my distorted features. How I picked up the utensils for the last time and examined them. One of the prongs on the fork was bent. So what. I stolidly placed the utensils, which I had once carefully selected from a huge basketful of olivewood utensils in the South of France, into the drawer. Let myself drop onto the kitchen chair. I guess the atom's not the only thing that's split around here . . .

Tears? Nerves, brother, whatever that may be. Only nerves. I wish that damned cloud would disperse or rain itself out or I don't know what. I wish your damned doctors would finally leave you alone. I wish everything was the way it used to be . . .

"And these signs shall follow them that believe: They shall take up serpents; and if they drink any deadly thing, it shall not hurt them . . ."

(And so one is already guilty, or shares in the guilt, by saying what one thinks, what one knows, and—although it may be hurtful—by feeling a certain satisfaction in the process. Because one knows it? Because one can say it? And remaining silent would be just as awful? What kind of a fix have we all got ourselves into, brother?)

". . . and as they stood there," said the man on the radio, "he was received up into heaven, a cloud took him off before their very eyes. Our preconceptions of time and space pale before the all-encompassing reality of God. This Christ went to the Father. That means he rules over us. The lords of this world go, our Lord cometh. Jesus Christ is the Lord. He shall come again. He shall render the world complete."

Fine, I answered the radio. But it wouldn't have had to be all that blunt. If, in fact, the need for rule and subordination is so pressing in us from early on

that it must form the basis of the invention of our gods—that we (I added, reflecting upon my life), should we be capable of freeing ourselves from the compulsion to worship gods, are prey to the compulsion to submit to people, ideas, idols—well, where then, brother heart, is the escape route (designated by white arrows against a green background in the hotels)? The emergency exit . . .

Man, was I tired, brother. The possibilities of distraction had exhausted themselves. I simply remained seated on the kitchen chair and did what I find most difficult: waiting. Of course I had no way of knowing in which of the many moments that form the length of such an operation, and none of which presumably is completely free of peril, the decision concerning your sense of smell was made. The olfactory cortex is one factor in the production of smells, along with the sensory cells in the nose, which weren't damaged, of course. Out of the three senses of distance of those reptilian dwellers of nocturnal niches—sight, hearing, and smell—it was smell which began to lose prominence when the mammals spread and became land-dwelling, daytime animals with the extinction of the reptiles. Since evolution—as opposed to technology, for example—does not destroy something once it has been created through selection, but rather finds further use for it, we have been left with the brain of snake and crocodile as one of our three brains. The ritual and hierarchical aspects of our lives are said to be strongly influenced by this R-complex, which, to a certain extent, still supposedly fulfills dinosaur functions in our brains: aggressive behavior, territoriality, the establishment of social hierarchies are partially controlled by it . . . Further along in the evolutionary process, when the closed groups appear, smell becomes absolutely essential as a means of differentiation (bees kill every foreign bee in their hive, which they recognize by their smell). There are a certain number of individuals among the human population for whom—as with their mammalian ancestors—the sense of smell plays a more important role in the initiation or intensification of sexual arousal than for others: this is the work of our second brain, the mammal in us, the limbic system, the components of which are the olfactory cortex and the pituitary gland; I am approaching the critical point with my thoughts and designations, brother. I am obliged to use an anatomical map of the brain to illustrate that which your surgeon sees before him. Strong emotions, powerful passions, and painful contradictions are said to originate in that sensitive region . . . Evolution probably no longer found it necessary to select human mutations that had broken the strong bond between smell and sexuality . . . So we won't mention it. Smell, brother, is one of those senses which, if I am not mistaken, are on the wane. It will take days before you miss it, on the tritest of occasions, when your aftershave has turned odorless. First you will be distracted by other, much more noticeable complaints. Those pathways of your neuron network whose function it was to handle smells, breaking them down into their components and letting certain points on that recognition pattern in your neocortex light up, which the latter then identified for you—violets, or: gas!—those pathways now lie fallow within you; the surgeon will hardly have enough time to shrug his shoulders apologetically, should he have noticed this, when severing the connection between the olfactory system and the neocortex. He still has the more ticklish tasks ahead of him in the region of the pituitary, where he must proceed in a manner both extremely cautious and extremely radical at once (the pituitary being the "master gland" which dominates the human endocrine system). He is aware of the irreparable consequences of any damages to the pituitary tissue and aware of the consequences of a timidity which would leave tumorous cells untouched within the healthy environment . . .

I suddenly noticed that my fingers were tightly clamped together, that I could hardly separate them, and that my shoulders and back ached. I jumped up and began to do limbering-up exercises. A melody came into my head then and after a while a few words turned up: ". . . My eyes dwelt long upon . . ." I couldn't come up with the entire text because a question kept pushing its way to the forefront of my thoughts: Where is Abel thy brother? Who's asking? Who faces up to this question of life and limb upon my inner stage? Who dares counter with the question: Am I my brother's keeper?

A Day's News

I stood rooted in the middle of the kitchen and for the first time I understood that the second, the counterquestioner, is not dissembling. Does not already know the answer. No. He stands there in the desert, deeply astounded, surprised, and asks: Am I my brother's keeper? That would be new. And, should the answer be yes!, dismaying enough. Whether Cain can simply carry on after that as before? Malevolent; envious; greedy for his birthright, that is to say: for the undivided love of the father and the embodiment thereof, possessions . . .

It is one in the afternoon, brother, what are they doing to you?

The telephone, not a second too soon. I hear that most important of all words: normal. Completely normal, did the nurse say? Really? We can stop worrying? The operation was a success? Oh. Really. I knew it. You, too? Of course he's not awake yet. That's the least of our concerns, don't you think? I heard you were doing well, brother, circumstances considered. I was prepared to bless the circumstances.

> . . . There was a cloud my eyes dwelt long upon
> It was quite white and very high above us
> Then I looked up, and found that it had gone.

Now I make myself something to eat. Can listen to the radio. In Sweden the radioactive contamination of the air had gone down further. And the contamination of the ground had gone up in turn.

But first I had to call up my friend. I told her what

I had just heard about my brother. Oh, good, she said. Very good. You're very close? He's the exact opposite of me, I said. We're close. She asked me what I was planning to do with my seeding now, and I said: If I only knew! We'll just have to become experts on half-life periods, she said. Do you have any idea what the half-life of cesium is, for example? Or strontium? I'm sure they'll fill us in on that, I said. Supposedly there are nuclids which require a hundred thousand years for their damned half-lives. At which point she said: Obscene, don't you think? and laughed in that demented way which otherwise occasionally irritates me. I was even gradually beginning to understand her laugh, I told her. Reality is catching up with my laugh, is that what you mean? she asked, and I said: More or less. Well, she said, they sure can't claim to have everything and every problem under control anymore. So maybe there's a good side to this as well, huh? Since we've got used to lopsided thinking, anyway? I wouldn't be so sure about that, I said. For some reason the belief in a technological solution to each and every problem kept being resurrected. Yes, she replied. And, by the way, did I also notice a certain wanton desire for those evil news reports every hour? A dark, malicious glee leveled at our own selves? I understood that, unfortunately, I said. You see, she said, that already made two. So maybe we should examine the whole situation from the point of view of our mutual guilt. That's asking quite a lot, I said. Mutual responsibility? she proposed. You said it, I replied.

A Day's News

... And yet that cloud had only bloomed for minutes
When I looked up, it vanished on the air.

Hopefully. Hopefully only minutes, was all I could
think, although this is a song from the time when
clouds were "white" and made of poetry and pure,
condensed vapor. But now, I thought while peeling
the boiled potatoes, it should be interesting to see
which poet would be the first to dare sing the praises
of a white cloud. An invisible cloud of a completely
different substance had seized the attention of our
feelings—completely different feelings. And, I thought
once again with that dark, malicious glee, it has
knocked the white cloud of poetry into the archives.
It has, in the space of a day, broken that and almost
every other spell.

Home fries. Egg sunny side up. Green salad. Milk.
"Simple foods taste best." Finally, my dear, your voice
breaks in as well. We'll need a day and a night to talk
over what we have learned this week. I won't reproach
you for going away from me at an inappropriate time.
Where you are now I hear that the pollutant emissions
following the reactor accident are more concentrated
than here. Should we be outraged? Uneasy? Should
we allow our feelings to become confused; worse still,
should we repress them as being insignificant? Insignificant values when measured with a Geiger counter?
I know what you're going to say. Don't say it. Starting
tomorrow, I have decided to cut down on milk and
avoid lettuce. Today I've resolved to eat and drink

everything one last time without a trace of bad conscience. That inner authority, which has been surfacing in me with ever increasing regularity, has begun, unasked, to calculate at what age the late sequelae of the last days' meals will catch up with me, should those meals contain radiating substances, the half-lives of which . . . At that point the silent, unwavering calculator in me inserted alternating values and I heard myself burst out laughing scornfully. Thirty years? Come now, dearest! And you honestly think you can scare me with that? The advantage of being older nowadays. Now tell me the truth: Would you want to be twenty today? ten? The horrified shudder within: Anything but that! That sufficed as test result for my intimate friend. I was allowed to eat in peace, wash the dishes. I heard on the radio that it was 1:45. And I saw myself standing there, the dish towel still in my hand, and heard myself singing at the top of my lungs. The Ode to Joy. Thy Shrine we tread, Thou Maid Divine. Now what is the meaning of this, I was forced to ask myself, somewhat flabbergasted. Joy! Joy . . .

Since I never would have been able to fathom this signal from the very deep layers of my consciousness otherwise, I decided to ask you later, brother, just when you actually awoke from the anesthetic that day which will then have become the past. 1:45? you will say. Wait a minute. Say, there's a good possibility . . . Yes. You could be right. Far off, all blurry, you were aware of the doctor's face above you and he probably had to scream his lungs out before you had understood his question: Can you see me? Can you see me! And you weren't able to answer no matter how hard you tried until you came up with the idea of opening and closing your eyes in response. He can see! you had heard. I can see, you will have whispered, still very hoarse, as the tube which they had had to insert into your windpipe for the anesthesia leaves the vocal cords sore; but they will heal. Yes, you will say, ever more clearly, and finally so loud that I will be able to hear it on the telephone, already tomorrow: I can see. And for days the word "see" will be present in all of its manifold and encompassing senses.

One day. One day is as a thousand years. A thousand years are as one day. How did the ancients know that? The smallest particles of matter, let loose, force us to handle the smallest particles of time with greater care. But now I'm tired, I heard myself say to me. Now I absolutely must lie down. I no longer wanted to hear that the first evacuations from the areas surrounding the rogue reactor had already begun at noontime on Saturday and had been completed within a few hours. I didn't want to have those pictures before my eyes as well that noon. "Evacuation," brother, is one of those words which we won't be able to separate from our own experience for the rest of our lives, I suppose. Sequences of images and emotions, melted down into an inseparable mass, are engraved upon the pathways of the brain. Once I was finally lying down, I tried to free myself from the stubborn image of how you must have been lying there, head bandaged, those tubes protruding from your veins. I also had no desire to imagine the inevitable pain; your thirst. I saw your shaven head before me, you were hardly more than a child, an unforgettable image in that typhoid hospital of the Mecklenburg town where we both lay and where our hair fell out after the typhoid fever.

I want to sleep now. I want some distraction, and that means reading. I looked around from where I lay on the bed and found that the book I would want to read on a day like this apparently had not yet been written. Who is it that locates the danger zone within a radius of precisely thirty kilometers, of all things, I thought to myself. Why thirty? Why always these even, round numbers? Why not twenty-nine? Or thirty-three? Would that be an admission that our calculations don't work out? That the natural and the unnatural don't obey our decimal system? There was no serious danger outside the immediate surroundings. And who decides how long people may be exposed to this serious danger? Can be exposed? Or must be? Who sets the danger boundaries, brother, within which we are supposed to live?

Everything I have been able to think and feel has gone beyond the boundaries of prose.

We cannot write the same way our brains work. If I had begun to resign myself to the seemingly unavoidable loss incurred on the nerve paths between the brain and the writing hand—it made a vivid reappearance in my consciousness that afternoon. Loss of immediacy, fullness, precision, focus, and a series of qualities I cannot define, perhaps do not even suspect. I could imagine circumstances which would leave me as well indifferent to a loss of this kind, because they will seem negligible when measured against the sacrifices which could then be demanded of us.

I wished that I could switch off my faculty of imagination. Those who conjure up the dangers above us and themselves must certainly be capable of that, I thought. Or don't they need to switch off anything; do they have a blind spot in their brains in the place of those premonitions which haunt the rest of us? One may not be able to pinpoint it like, say, the centers of appetite, balance, temperature control, circulation, breathing. So one couldn't stimulate that blind spot with electrical impulses in the same way that a certain neurologist by the name of Penfield activated memory traces in the cerebral cortexes of his patients by conducting electricity through them. Sounds. Colors. A smell from the past. A composition for orchestra with all its intricacies. I could not help thinking with uneasiness (aren't we good students, brother!) that one could let human beings live for a certain amount of time—twenty years? twenty-five?—let them lead a normal, yes, an exceptionally rich human life, the objective being to fill their memory banks "to the brim." Afterwards these beings would be led or abandoned to the vocation intended for them in the first place: a dreary existence in some mechanical installation, a subterranean missile site, a spaceship. And a specialist would hook them up to the memory currents during their prescribed recreation intervals. Love. Enmity. Success. Failure. Tenderness. Conflict. Natural beauty—they would relive everything as intensely as they could, over and over again. They could not fall victim to the deadly boredom of their "real" existence. The wish to die rather than continue leading such a life could not gain a hold over them. Their brains would have connived against them behind their backs (how disproportionate language is becoming!), together with their manipulators. Objects of the most wretched kind, they would . . .

These are the kinds of fantasies I would strictly forbid myself, brother, if I had the means to realize them. I wouldn't even dare to articulate them, barely think them. In our century there is only a paper-thin wall separating a technological fantasy in the mind from its realization?

Yet this is not the stuff of which are made the sins with which we would have to reproach ourselves, or I myself. We have not said too much—rather, too little—and that little bit too timidly and too late. And why? For banal reasons. Because of insecurity. Because of fear. Because of lack of hope. And, strange as the claim may be: because of hope as well. Deceitful hope, which produces the same results as paralyzing despair.

I read that the connection between murder and invention has been with us as long as agriculture itself.

Cain, tiller of the soil and inventor? The founder of civilization? It was difficult to refute the hypothesis that human beings were the most important tool in the selection which brought about a speedy further development of the brain through battles against their own kind and the extermination of inferior groups. Those mutations whose aggressions were freely directed against members of their own species (deemed unfavorable in the selection process of most animal species) led to further evolution of the "king of beasts"—relatively superior to other enemies on account of his intelligence. Murder within one's own species as a way of preventing overpopulation? Murder within limits, biologically acceptable? And thus did man become his own enemy?

I put the book aside and reached for something else, a periodical. There was an article which someone had recommended that I read, not without inducing in me a fear of it at the same time. A certain somebody who isn't even here now, where he belongs, especially today; who is exposing himself to the higher radiation—apparently! a coincidence—of distant places instead, still further evidence that even short-term separations are best avoided nowadays. At whom I got furious, but whom I still did not want to call, so that my voice would not worry him, as I would not be able to put on a front in such a way that he would not be able to see through it immediately (four "nots" in one sentence). That was what he got for having me read this article all alone, unprotected and still furious, in a fit of sad courage and masochism, for its title was already encouraging enough: The scientists of "Star Wars." My fear of the article quickly proved justified; however it then shifted to those very young scientists with whom it dealt and whom he referred to as "star warriors." A word which triggered a signal within me I could still ignore. Highly gifted, very young men who—driven, I fear, by the hyperactivity in certain centers of their brains—have not signed a pact with the devil (oh, brother! the good old devil! would that he still existed!), but rather with the fascination with a technical problem. Only gradually did I realize, as the description helped form a picture of their lives in my mind, that the fantasies I had forbidden myself earlier on had long since been surpassed by reality: these were, in fact, men in an isolation ward, without women, without children, without friends, without any other pleasures apart from their work, subjugated to the strictest of safety and security regulations; but they didn't need any substitute life of electrically produced memories. How naïve I still was! All they evidently needed was a pseudo-relationship to absorb their emotions. But of course, no problem. Why do we have computers. By the time of their arrival (I refrain from saying "admission") at their Star Wars laboratory, Livermore, they are probably already done for. They know not father nor mother, I have read. Not brother nor sister. Not woman nor child (there are no women there, brother heart! is this oppressive fact the cause of young people's love of com-

puters? or the effect?). What they do know, these mere
children with their highly trained brains, with the restless left hemispheres of their brains working feverishly
night and day—what they do know is their machine.
Their lovely, beloved computer. To which they are
bound, shackled, as only ever a slave to his galley.
Nourishment: peanut-butter sandwiches. Hamburg-
ers with ketchup. Coke from the fridge. What they
do know is the objective to construct the nuclear-
powered X-ray laser at the core of that fantasy of an
America rendered totally secure through the reloca-
tion of future nuclear battles to outer space. (What
are they: legitimate descendants of that scientist ob-
sessed with "the truth," a myth familiar to us all?—
or the illegitimate offspring who use his name in vain?
Shall obsession be a fault? "ordinary life" a value in
itself?) The signal within me became louder, I had to
lower my journal. Why did I have the feeling that I
knew what they were talking about? Star warriors.
Star Wars . . . Of course! Once, almost exactly three
years ago, we sat in a crowded movie theater just a
few miles from that Livermore National Laboratory
on the West Coast of the U.S.A. in Berkeley, Califor-
nia, watching, at first with embarrassed astonishment
and then with growing uneasiness, the sequel to *Star
Wars*, whose title I would soon remember if I just
didn't think too hard. At first I couldn't help but think
of the young black woman sitting right behind me,
fanatically participating in the space battles of the
good white star warriors versus the evil black ones,

(63

along with the rest of the theater. I could still hear
the young black woman screaming shrilly at one cli-
mactic moment: Kill him! Kill him! And I realized:
the weapons being used there were indeed nuclear
weapons, and I imagined that the director of these
two films, who had, of course, become incredibly rich
off them (*The Return of the Jedi*, yes, that was the
name of the film), had consulted with the star warriors
in Livermore; or they with the film people. And all
of them with the politicians . . . And I understood:
'tis not the phantom "security"—no: 'tis the mael-
strom of death, the fabrication of the void, which
herds some of the best brains in America.

Anyway, the Faust of that article to which I returned as under compulsion was called Peter Hagelstein, not Frankenstein. Gretchen: Josie—Josephine
Stein. Peter is a runner, swimmer, plays the piano and
flute, loves French literature, suffers from insomnia
and depressions and can't cope with everyday life. He
works fourteen, fifteen hours a day, "seven days a
week." His goal of winning the Nobel Prize for the
invention of an X-ray laser for scientific purposes is
turned around in Livermore. Hagelstein–Faust actually hates bombs. Josie–Gretchen is a firm supporter
of that hatred. She begins joining the demonstrators
who appear before the gates of Livermore. In a state
of exhaustion and lack of control, Hagelstein–Faust
lets one of his ingenious ideas slip out: a single bomb
as the driving mechanism of different devices for the
creation of an X-ray laser. They then get him to work

out the precise calculations through political pressure. Which he doesn't really want to do. Josie protests. Then she splits up with Peter. His experiment, which proves superior to those of others, took place as early as 1980. And there we were in 1983 sitting in that movie theater, completely in the dark.

A Faust who does not seek to win knowledge but rather fame. A Gretchen who wishes rather to redeem him than be destroyed by him . . . I would reflect upon the new Faust–Gretchen variation later. I felt a chill within me which, as in the past on certain occasions, has a tendency to spread. I know of no defense against people who are secretly addicted to death. The rats. Once again the image of those rats which had been trained to stimulate their centers of desire by pressing a button. They love that button. Press, press, press. At the risk of starving, perishing of thirst, becoming extinct.

At which crossroads did human evolution possibly go so wrong that we have coupled the satisfaction of our desires with the compulsion to destroy. Or, put another way, what fear is it that insulates those young men so reliably against that which we normal people call "life." A fear which must be so immense that they would rather "free" the atom than themselves . . . My sleep continued to puzzle restlessly over the question of where my own responsibility lay, circumnavigating the blind spot which my words, try as they might, do not wish to know. Are not allowed to know . . .

During your first sleep after the operation you

dreamed, brother, that you were falling, falling, falling—from high up, apparently unstoppable. And that you then, rather than being smashed to bits upon impact as fearfully anticipated, landed softly in a huge pile of hay. Thus did our distant forebears, the tree-dwelling primates, firmly inscribe within us the fear of falling. It is our earliest childhood fear, brother, fear incarnate, and the fact that it was released within you on that day is not all that hard to understand. In my dream, on the other hand, I was with our grandparents in a narrow room in which there was little except old wooden beds, and I was sitting on the edge of a bed next to our Grandmother Marie and put my arm around her shoulders because her husband, our Grandfather Gottlieb, had supposedly just died, but she didn't seem very sad (indeed, in reality she died before him), and somehow this deceased grandfather was also back again, and our other two grandparents were sitting opposite us and we were talking about how big Grandfather Gottlieb's pension might have been in the end, and Grandmother Marie said quietly: The largest possible pension, 130 marks. I got very sad but the atmosphere in the room was peaceful, intimate, although the two pairs of grandparents hadn't been that close at all in life, and I felt secure with them, safe and protected, and I also had the feeling that they wanted to give me knowledge, and as I awoke I thought: They wanted to tell me that we all have to die and that we can accept it. For the space of a moment I understood that our lives lead up to such simple truths and I felt gratitude toward my grandparents and all the forebears who had struggled through life before me, and before them, but that feeling disappeared very quickly. I made my afternoon coffee, drank it, heard that, so far, the reactor catastrophe had claimed no more than two lives; I heard the voices whose doubts concerning that figure approached disdain, and the others, who wished to consider it realistic.

It suddenly seemed impossible for me to further put off transplanting the Japanese peace flowers from their pots, where I had let them winter, to the flower bed. Surely there was no more night frost to be expected; the year before, I had received the advice, together with the plants, that the small plants would have to toughen up and then they would also stand their ground in our climate. A Japanese soldier had brought this flower home from the Japanese war against Burma, planted it as a peace symbol, since then it had spread all over Japan; one wished that it would make its home in Europe, too. Conscious of my responsibility toward these test plants, I carefully planted the seedlings in a free spot in the flower bed. (Only one of them held out into this cold autumn. From its seed I am trying to breed descendants in pots which, for their part, could winter in a protected environment. An activity which needs no justification.)

. . . as it goes without saying, I should hope that in some deep recesses of your body, brother, healing powers are now being produced incessantly and channeled into those regions where they are most needed. That doesn't mean only your head, not only the wound, which is probably already now beginning to pulsate and hurt. I doubt that you're already thinking. That center in which thought and language are coupled will still be dusky. The centers of sound formation which are primarily hidden in the gray cavity of the midbrain in subhuman primates . . .

Suddenly I felt a powerful desire to move around, went to the stable again, got out the bicycle, and, pedaling firmly, although out of shape, conquered the small slope leading up to the little transformer house, felt my heart pounding, my pulse racing with satisfaction, and then shot down the narrow paved street toward the neighboring village. To my right and to my left, I saw that there would be wheat this year as far as the eye could see, my eyes would not be able to get their fill of the different shades of the ripe grain; this day which I not only had to get through but had to live out hour by hour would be memory. In the next village I met only children in the street, they called after me, I didn't look back, seldom does a stranger on a bicycle come through this remote village. At the exact moment when I passed the sign marking the village limits, the first jet fighter broke the sound barrier directly overhead, or so it seemed; as I am incapable of getting used to them, I was once again frightened to the bone, ducked down, and rode on as fast as possible to reach the shelter of the woods, while the formation of fighter jets from the new airfield

nearby carried out its training program. I have long
since reconciled myself to the fact that the fear of
airplanes diving down at me in a spray of machine-
gun fire, dating back to the last days of the war, will
never leave me; bathed in sweat I reached the edge of
the woods, turned off the street and onto the narrow,
bumpy path, which demanded all my attention until
I reached the spot to the right of which lie our dancing
stones. I put my bike down beside the path and walked
the thirty, forty meters across the springy forest soil.
There stood the stones. Nine primeval upright field-
stones, in a perfect circle beneath ancient beeches—
later, in a green twilight in midsummer with its dense
foliage; at the moment, since the beeches are only just
beginning to turn green, in a merely slightly filtered
light unfamiliar to me. We know why we come back
to this spot again and again and stand at the edge or
in the middle of the circle marked out by the stones.
We are searching for the secret. Even if these stones
were not erected in those gray days of prehistory
(" . . . In the central gray cavity of the midbrain are
hidden . . .") but in later centuries—we do not want
to know. We want to imagine that our very early
ancestors needed precisely these stones, arranged in
this pattern at precisely this spot, to perform their—
bloody? unbloody?—ceremonies, with whose help
they ensconced and legitimized themselves in their
conviction of the superiority, indeed the universal
validity, of their nature. We have, in the light of our
own territorial ceremonies and edifices, ceased call-

ing this "wild." The brains of those members of a tribe who may have danced, researched, sacrificed here were no more primitive than our own. No one nowadays conceives of the transition to Homo sapiens in terms of a "leap." For about a hundred thousand years the size of the brain stood in colossal disproportion to the performance demanded of it. Harassed by an overdeveloped, exceedingly active nervous system, these early humans, banished from the animal kingdom, had to turn this harassment into an advantage: into the compulsion to make human beings of themselves. Today this place is called "Dry Jug" by the local people, a name handed down from the times of the wagoners who, on their way to Poland along the nearby old northern German salt road, stopped here to rest: a dry rest, this jug was empty . . .

The rank growth of the brain may have been as much of a hindrance as a help for the ancestors of Homo sapiens throughout a long period of prehistory. Those stones, brother, those dances and ceremonies, helped them develop a cultural apparatus, forms with which to envelop their humanity. What we call customs . . .

It was quite still by the dancing stones; I stood there a long time leaning against the largest stone and surrendering to the images which always overcome me here. The woods smelled deeply of springtime. You know that one can't describe smells. It must have been at about that time that the head surgeon came to your bed and, seeing that you were awake, spoke to you of how the operation had gone, which you, however, could not comprehend, unable as you were to concentrate. This time you managed a clear, if somewhat hoarse "Yes!" in response to his repeated, insistent question: Can you see me?, which seemed to please him no end, indeed, to relieve him; you, on the other hand, were reassured by the statement which he repeated until it gained admission to your sluggish and grudgingly operative information apparatus: As far as it is humanly possible to tell, we have removed everything which was harmful.

I can only hope that the fragrance of the woods in springtime is firmly anchored in your memory. *How fares my child / how fares my fawn* . . . I went a little farther through the woods and looked for signs of disease on the trees, but couldn't find any. That we should have the choice only of living with radioactivity or with the dying woods led me, when we once discussed it, to make exaggerated or, as you put it, overblown remarks. Remarks about our being caught between false alternatives. In that case, I heard you say, I would have to be prepared to do without my creature comforts. *How fares my child / how fares my fawn / two times I'll come and then nevermore.* Can it be true: have our own wishes brought us to this? Has the idle, oversized part of our brain fled into manic-destructive hyperactivity, faster and faster and, finally—today—at breakneck speed, hurling out ever new fantasies, which we, unable to stop ourselves, have turned into objectives of desire and entrusted to our machine world in the form of production tasks?

Getting back was more difficult, riding against the wind, which had risen during the afternoon. To the left, at the edge of the wood, I now saw the herd of deer grazing in the grain seed. *How fares my child / how fares my fawn / once again I'll come and then nevermore.* At last my memory figured out where this passage comes from, who says it, and how that entire memory is connected with the basic pattern of this day. I had to laugh out loud. Little Brother and Little Sister. That fairy tale transported us to unfathomable depths of sadness when we were children and yet we always felt compelled to come back to it. Off we set, into the wilderness, again and again, hand in hand, turned out by the wicked stepmother, and the springs from which you wanted to drink: *I'm thirsty, Little Sister. If I knew of a spring I'd go and get a drink. Listen! I think I can hear one running* . . . the springs warned us with their babbling voices, which I translated for you: Little Brother, don't drink it, otherwise you'll turn into a wild beast and tear me to pieces. That was always the point where my heartrending sadness set in, and often, often did I try to talk you out of your thirst, but we both knew how the story went, didn't we, and we couldn't do anything to change it. You went crazy with thirst and kept on pleading for a sip of water, until, wailing and moaning, I was forced to let you drink from the last spring. It was the faucet in our kitchen, and then you turned into a deer, as we had been warned, which was bad enough, but still better than if you had turned into a tiger or a wolf and had torn me to pieces. I put a ribbon around your neck, just as in the fairy tale, and led you, little deer, all through the apartment, which was a dense, impenetrable forest, and we were terribly frightened, until we found shelter under the table, where we both wished to live together in peace, Little Brother and Little Sister. It was a dire fate that one should either die of thirst or turn into a wild beast, and often, often did I reproach you, Little Brother, that I, Little Sister, could manage to restrain myself; that I, although as thirsty as you, did not have to drink at all costs. But you did have to drink at all costs and you had to go out into the forest at the sound of the hunt, in spite of my tears and pleadings, and so it was you who led the unknown prince right up to our refuge, whom I didn't want to have for a husband at all, for I only wanted you, Little Brother, even as a deer, and we lay awake at night and asked ourselves in whispers whether it was humanly possible that our mother was a stepmother as well in reality, and we swore to each other never, never to let anybody separate us, but one night you asked me whether I wasn't the false sister whom the wicked, envious stepmother had foisted on the king without his or anybody else's noticing a thing, and then I had to resort to the most powerful formula we knew, kept for the most pressing of emergencies. May I drop dead if I'm not the real sister. Upon which you were silent for a little while, Little Brother, and then asked cautiously: Have you dropped dead? And I said with a sad, sad heart: No. And thus had been proven that which should never have needed proving. *How fares my child / how fares my fawn* . . . Oh, this early susceptibility to sad verse. This early fear of the dark side of our nature, from which we can never liberate ourselves except through death and destruction. The false sister was taken into the forest, where the wild beasts tore her to pieces; the witch was put in the fire and suffered a miserable death by burning. And when she was reduced to ashes the little fawn was transformed and once again took on his human shape. So Little Sister and Little Brother lived happily together to the end of their days.

The day remained flawless up to its final minute. The sun was still two hands above the horizon as I came back into the village, past the little transformer house, pushing my bicycle after all, since I couldn't make the hill; the contours had become sharper toward evening, the colors even richer. One can't know how many shades of green there are before having been here. Before the village houses, left and right, the old leftover women sat, each one by herself, their gouty hands clasped in their laps, heads bent, staring at the ground in front of them. They barely acknowledged my greeting. Will the village be empty in a few years?

As I rode between the two mighty lime trees onto our property, I noticed a small cluster of people stand-

ing in the meadow in front of the house. As I drew
nearer, I saw that it was a family, husband, wife,
nearly grown-up daughter. I could tell by the way they
looked around and then set off in the direction of the
garden that they were looking for something, and
suppressed a strong displeasure at their presence. I
leaned my bicycle against the wall of the stable and
crossed the meadow after them. I asked if they were
looking for anything in particular; they turned with
a start, and the man—I guessed that he was about
fifty—explained to me, slightly embarrassed, that he
had lived in a room of this house with his mother and
brothers and sisters as a refugee back in '45. Yes: this
must have been the house, he repeated quizzically, as
if I could confirm it for him: this slightly elevated
spot. The lime trees. The stone stairs with the railings
right and left, leading to a porch . . . And the village,
there he was quite certain, it was the same village. Of
course he had been a child back then, but certain
things had been indelibly engraved upon his memory,
and since they lived on the coast, not all that far away,
they had finally set out to show their daughter all of
this. But, to be perfectly honest, he had yet another
reason for coming here. He believed that his little
sister had been buried on this land back then, after
dying of typhoid fever. They had all had typhoid back
then. Yes, I said, that's true. I know that for a fact.
But, although anyone who refers to the typhoid epi-
demic in the first year after the war can count on my
sympathy, I was nonetheless annoyed at this man.

What gave him the right to presume the remains of his little sister here, on our property; how dare he tell me such a thing. I had not the slightest desire to know who had possibly been buried here forty years ago, rolled up in a blanket or simply stuck in a cardboard box, I did not want to know that his sister's name had been Anneliese, that she had been only three years old, and that they just didn't have anything for her to eat, I know those stories, I was there, you wasted away to skin and bones, brother, in the typhoid hospital in H., where I was taken before you, I almost didn't recognize you when I finally managed the thirty steps down the corridor to your room, now this man with his little olive-green coat should leave me alone with his sister Anneliese, I came here in search of peaceful slumber, I don't need his descriptions of starving little girls. I just didn't want to hear it. I almost rudely interrupted the man, who had suddenly, and, to all appearances, unexpectedly, been moved to tears by memory. I told him that the cemetery was so close by, barely a hundred meters, that it was highly unlikely that a child would not be buried there but on the parson's private property. The man was slightly shaken. If you think so, he said, and was there still a parson whom one could possibly ask. No, I said, the church might be a historic monument, but it was no longer a functioning house of worship, the parson was very young and lived in a neighboring village, hardly anyone would be able to tell him anything about '45. I thought to myself, if he really cared about his sister he wouldn't have had to wait forty years, at the same time I understood that there could have been a sort of gap in this man's life in which the face and the tiny form of his starved sister had suddenly reappeared. But I couldn't help him there, and, to my relief, the trio walked off toward the cemetery. I turned around and saw the house against the light, as the sun had already slipped behind the roof, and its face, which had always seemed friendly to me up till then, was twisted in an ugly grimace. Since I had cured myself of giving in to sudden changes of mood, I interpreted this in actual fact truly horrible feeling as being due to physical and mental exhaustion and went straight into the house. But I couldn't get that moment out of my mind, even though I have long known that all skin can tear open and the monsters well up out of those tears. That the structure behind the façades tends to collapse from time to time; that entire stretches love to drop out of the road, right at our feet, into the yawning abyss.

Unfortunately, I thought as I began to wander about the house, unfortunately my early childhood was geared toward rooting in me the conviction that my own well-being and the ways of the world are bound together in a benevolent manner; and when that little sister, who perhaps lies buried, after all, somewhere on the land which my eyes were now scanning from the windows of the house, fell easy prey to the typhoid for lack of food, I was already over the worst; true, history lay broken in pieces, I did not see how the pieces could be put together again; however, perhaps because I had been old enough to work for potatoes and milk, the typhoid did not come up against a weakened body and wasn't of the deadly kind—the same went for you, brother. We were lucky back then and many times before and since, and although I do know that does not give us a right to luck, I still seem to assume that there is such a thing as an established right to luck,

and so I wasn't lying when I assured you that I firmly believed your operation would be successful. Wasn't lying and wasn't being completely honest. However, at one point, my passionate contradiction and my anger were genuine through and through; namely, when you were about to start saying that life had given you all it could—from now on, it could only repeat itself. At which point I stormed at my own most secret thoughts with anger and conviction,

as I now stormed at the wife of the man in the little olive-green coat who, upon walking away, had said: Who knows what your sister was spared. That same Anneliese who, if she had to be buried on this property at all, would most likely be lying beneath the old walnut tree, would have been forty-five years old now, and I began inventing her a life while counting up all the places in the house where electricity was used, coming to the conclusion that there were too many and beginning to contemplate the ways in which we could noticeably lower our consumption. The small radio that I was carrying around in my arm ran on batteries. It informed me, as I was going from window to window in the attic, taking in the incomparable views of which one never tires—it informed me that in Kiev the mothers or grandmothers were starting to leave the city with the children, and I had to imagine that these were children who, for their part, in spite of all they might have learned about the war which had swept across their city once in what was for them the gray, distant past, had been able to develop a feeling of invulnerability and that now, without their knowing, the lives of some of them—superstitious fear kept the count as low as possible, even in my thoughts—would be marked by the aftermath of a mere accident, the consequences of pure chance.

Why is it that we can't bear being the victims of chance. I sat down at my desk to finally read the morning mail, among other things a letter from that woman, over eighty years old, who writes to me from London in her generous, aged handwriting, and whom I would so much like to see—a wish I nourish within me without yielding too much to the doubts that stir within me the longer her illness, we both say "exhaustion," lasts. Fear of old age? she wrote. Fear of waning intensity, joy of living, resilience? But that was a lot of nonsense. And wasn't it so much more reasonable to abandon oneself to the rhythm of work, exhaustion, rest, and rely upon those powers within us which naturally strive toward renewal. Toward rebirth.

What a word. Are you listening in, brother: rebirth.

Yes, I could quite well remember the times when I myself used such words and they had a meaning for me. A quick, sharp pain of longing tore open all those times before me, together with the abyss into which they had disappeared. I realized that at some point—perhaps not all at once, perhaps definitively only today—the ropes fastening our life net to certain fixtures had snapped. Ropes which could be called not only safeguards but also bonds. Those before us would forever be supported and bound by them; those after us have cut the ropes and consider themselves released, free to do and not to do as they please. Never again would we be able to rely on those ties, nor would we ever be completely rid of them, if only in our longing for them. The mere accident of her being Jewish had driven her out of Hitler's Berlin, my London correspondent wrote to me. She would never have made that decision of her own free will, deeply rooted among colleagues and friends, hungry for closeness, warmth, approval as she was. Imagine a doctor, a psychologist in a foreign-language community. And it turned out as she had predicted: she had never felt at home anywhere again. Yet, since then, every moment of her life had taxed her to the limit, every few years she had had to think up a new sphere of work for herself. So that the evil which had driven her into exile more than half a century earlier had ever so gradually transformed itself into a fortunate act of fate for her within the course of her long life.

It was she, I thought, she alone who had trans-

formed the evil. It occurred to me that, in my search
for the roots of our desire for destruction, I could
consult her book on the human hand, which stood
within casy reach on the shelf . . .

I know your hands by heart, brother, can picture
them at any time. I assume they are getting thinner
and, in a way which is hard to describe, older. I think
I can imagine how they are resting there on the blanket, the only thing with which you reveal your identity, since your head is bandaged, ill, defenseless,
unconscious. Often, often did we place our hands next
to one another on a piece of paper, you the right one,
I the left, each of us tracing an outline of them with
our free hands. Your hands gradually caught up to
mine in size, but their outlines remained so different that one doesn't have to be an expert to read
the different personalities and inclinations in our
palms . . .

I read in the book that the human hand develops
that web of highly significant lines distinguishing it,
for example, from the hand of the simian. Once again,
as fascinated as the first time, I studied illustrations
of the hands of apes, all of which show no individual
characteristics but are marked by the "simian line"
alone, cutting across the palm horizontally—a sight
which once again filled me with melancholy, as if the
ape were trapped in creatural sadness over its failed
evolution into a human being. As if it held out its
palms to us as a symbol of this sadness and a helpless
plea for our sympathy. The prehuman may also have

(8 1

approached another member of its horde with hands raised to symbolize peaceful intentions before it could speak. Yet only with the help of language, which soon, that is to say, after hundreds of thousands of years, complemented those gestures of aggression and humility, liberated us from a dependence on our instincts and once and for all awarded us superiority over the animals—with the help of language, of all things, did the humans of one horde seem to have dissociated themselves from those of another horde: the one who spoke differently was the other, was not human, was not subject to the murder taboo. This idea comes at an awkward moment. Language which creates identity but which, at the same time, makes a decisive contribution to the dismantling of the inhibition about killing that member of the species who speaks differently. The same language which marks the leap to "complete humanity" widening consciousness, thereby forcing the hitherto conscious into the unconscious: thus, "When the sun sets we are able to perceive the stars. In the same way, the brilliance of our most recent evolutionary accretion, the verbal abilities of the left hemisphere, obscures our awareness of the functions of the intuitive right hemisphere, which in our ancestors must have been the principal means of perceiving the world." The Janus face of language . . .

My old London friend, my namesake (a coincidental circumstance which brought us together), died, as I know now, on the same day that I began to write about her. So, exhausted after all. So, forever whisked out of range of my wish to see her just one time. I have before me one of her first books, in German translation. (One should not underestimate the language barrier, she once wrote to me.) Again I read the description of her first days as an immigrant in England, her barely concealed despair at the futility of communication—a deplorable state of affairs which apparently could not be remedied by her ever improving English because it lay beneath the layer of language, and I picked up her last book, which arrived on the same day as her last letter; it is written in English like her autobiography, in which I came across the sentences: "But in the social plight of our age we have to reconcile ourselves to half measures. We are forced to use our multiple personalities like players acting different plays. We have to hide our authentic Self under a mask, and act a part in order to come to terms with a stereotyped social code." Is this so? So it is. In writing, brother—since you ask—we are more and more obliged to act the part of the writer and, by falling out of character, to pull off our masks, to let our authentic self shimmer through, between the lines which follow the social code, whether we want to or not. We are mostly blind to this process. A day like this, paradoxical in its repercussions, forces us, forces me to make the personal public, to overcome reluctance.

In the large envelope which I opened last there were texts selected by Swiss women to be exhibited as posters on the anniversary of Hiroshima. I wasn't really surprised that they were texts on the subject of the "confusion of tongues"—accustomed as I was to the fact that, in certain pressing situations, everything falls into place. "And the whole earth was of one language and of one speech," I read, and it seemed as if I were reading this ancient text for the first time. "And they said, Go to, let us build us a city and a tower, whose top may reach unto heaven . . ." THE LORD seems to be very sensitive on the subject of hubris. He descends promptly and speaks: "Behold, the people is one, and they have all one language; and this they begin to do; and now nothing will be restrained from them, which they have imagined to do." At which point he confuses their tongues and thus prevents the building of the tower, as we all know. Interestingly enough, he uses the same means in the case of the megalomaniac Emperor Nimrod: he, too, has a tower built, a shining symbol of his presumption, a tower so high already "that it took an entire year before the slime and the bricks did reach the mason at the top." But while they were building, "they shot arrows into the heavens, and the arrows fell back bloody. And one did speak to the other: Now have we killed all that is up above. But this was the work of the LORD that they be confounded and wiped off the face of the earth. And this he did by confounding their language that they may not understand one another's speech." How seriously THE LORD takes language. How he makes certain that it does not become an instrument which serves his subjects to join forces against him. We, on the other hand, all understand the basic language with which we build our towers, I couldn't help thinking, but that doesn't do us any good; and we all recognize the technological voice coming out of a machine, and we join in the countdown when it sends that other machine, the rocket-powered tower, into the sky, which is no longer called the sky, by the way, but the cosmos: five—four—three—two—one— ZERO! Only sometimes the towers come crashing down, with their bloody cargo . . .

This was one of those days during which all the signs we have been shown up to now come to mind without my understanding them. I sat down and wrote you a letter, brother, in large print for the sake of your still weakened eyes, using expressions like "new beginning" and "rebirth," making myself believe in them, although I wondered whether I don't keep insisting on them out of defiance or out of my incapability to truly face the new situation, or whether I merely thought it appropriate to strengthen your will to recover, even through a bit of deception. I briefly thought of the connection between the word "deception"—or, better still, "self-deception"—and the "blind spot" around which I had been circling, drawing ever nearer,

but first I arranged before me the four or five other letters, containing queries or invitations, and answered them, the latter in the negative. I kept looking outside while doing so. I did not want to miss the sunset, ran up to the attic when the sun was just two fingers above the horizon, watching it set for ten, fifteen minutes in a play of colors known only to northern skies, and of which I can never get my fill. That sunsets would not bore me, even when more and more of that which I still consider important today had become indifferent to me, or meaningless (as so much of what used to be important ten years, and more still from twenty years ago, no longer interests me today)—this thought was a small consolation. Incidentally, the blood-red ball of the sun seemed a very distant, foreign, and unapproachable star to me that day, as its outermost edge touched the outermost edge of the earth, which appeared to rise up a few millimeters to meet it, and I could not understand how people could ever write poetry about it and, even less, how one could sing to it: *"Sweet evening sun / Thou art so beautiful."* Half a century ago I heard my grandmother sing that in her kitchen. For no apparent reason, the sight of this star strengthened my conviction on that evening that we are alone in space and no human signal will respond to us, no matter how high or how far we may shoot our rocket towers and other probes. Why on earth send those space plaques with the contours of a human couple—the man's hand raised in a greeting of peace—in our spacecraft, as a message to humanoid creatures on other planets, if those who invented and produced them are no longer capable of entering their neighbor's house and eliciting a human signal, a smile . . .

A Day's News

Should cerebral damage impair the language centers, the remaining personality would also be disturbed if other parts of the brain did not—as sometimes happened—take over this special function. Now we can think such sentences freely and openly, brother, can't we. The number and the kinds of thinkable sentences are generally increasing by the hour, since I know that you are alive; you remain the one we know. "Deprived," I hear you say, but what does that mean. Deprived of that capability to regulate stress which the suprarenal gland must take over at a signal from the pituitary. The signal does not come, the suprarenal gland does not begin to work, the hormone is missing, you cannot regulate situations of stress beyond a certain level. You are permitted, however, within those confines, to work five hours a day in a concentrated fashion. Who else is able to do that! Are not our expectations too high, or pointed in the wrong direction. Is it not possibly your task now to relax, let yourself go; enjoy that which can be obtained without exerting yourself. And not: continually to incite those areas of your nervous system which might have been "trying" to suggest to you, through the disease, to take it easy on them.

But that is no life.

It isn't?

A life devoid of eight hours' intensive work a day is no life. Words such as "invalid" creep in should the standard of performance no longer be up to par. Language does its bit, rashly delivering the terms and consolidating a rather vague feeling. And how can one get away from, and get out from under, certain words now that they have been pronounced and are out in the open? Even if this has, so far, not been a problem for you, brother—it will be a problem now. So that your range of experience is surely widening in a certain sense, as I keep trying to tell you. Taking in undesired areas, perhaps. So that it would now be your task to accept those undesired experiences and finally, if possible, to see them as desirable . . .

But that is really asking too much.

As I was taking the letters to the mailbox, it struck me: unreasonable demands always seem to relate to omissions in unlived zones of life and cannot easily be rectified by life lived later. What's gone is gone; the older we get, the more we learn to respect and fear the inexorability of time. One can rack one's brains in search of justifications for things left undone, such as: but instead of that, I worked, wrote. No use. The omission stakes its claim in the form of guilt and is not to be undone . . .

Now we're getting close, very close, to our blind spot after all. Whether it was actually a requirement of nature, whether there was no other solution to the construction of the human eye than to equip it with a blind spot, that tiny point in the retina where it is joined by the optic nerve, leading to the brain. Speedy consolation. Our other eye is said to compensate for this minimal gap in our perception. But who or what can help us fill that gap in our perception which we inevitably inflict upon ourselves through our special way of holding our own in this world? Where to find consolation for this?

Brotherliness—that word was due. Joined in brotherhood, unified in brotherhood, brotherly salutes. We no longer want to know of the embittered battle among brothers. Our silent, unrelenting battles in the nursery. Big sister dislocates little brother's shoulder. Unspeakable disgrace that a mother's children should not love one another dearly. It will be your fault if his arm stays stiff. Original guilt. The original crime, which can be committed only against the brother, the sister. Mother and father, whose love actually sparks off the fight, withdraw behind an even stronger taboo. Infinite gratitude to the brotherly arm doing us the favor of not staying stiff. At least not this time. This time there is only the warning, which we must take to heart. Relieved, we take it to heart. Force the passions leading to the tough, embittered battles with the brother down into the crater in our selves, which has developed early enough as the final disposal site for unbearable radioactive feelings. What is the use of constantly keeping an eye on it.

The blind spot.

The heart of darkness.

That sounds good, but something in me remains dissatisfied. Where, I thought, would the blind spot have to be situated within me, in my brain—should it be possible to localize it, after all. Language. Speaking, formulating, articulating. Would not the center of greatest desire have to be located in close proximity to that darkest point? The peak alongside the crater?

Language. Speaking. It is worth coming back to that. I sense the agitated flickering at the blurred edges of my consciousness. Once a species has begun to speak, it can no longer do without. Language is not one of those gifts which can be accepted experimentally, on trial. It represses many of our animal instincts. We cannot fall back on them—never! We have pushed off from the animal kingdom for good. The infant that comes into the world equipped with archaic reflexes must cast them off within a few weeks in order to be able to develop normally; into a human being, that is. The frontal lobes of the neocortex have assumed command. Civilization is their product. Language, the medium of tradition, their prerequisite.

What is nagging me, then? Suspicion, self-distrust. My brain, receptive to language beyond what is normal, must be programmed by this and no other medium to assert the values of this civilization. It is probably not even possible for me to formulate those questions which could lead me to radical answers. The light of language has pushed into the dark entire regions of my inner world, which may have lain in twilight during prelanguage times. I do not remember. At some point, or many points, we have had to include that savagery, folly, bestiality in civilization, which was created only to tame the untamed. The reptile in us slaps its tail. The wild animal in us roars. Our features distorted, we rush at the brother and kill him.

A Day's News

Then we wish to tear the brains out of our heads and search for the savage spot that we may burn it out. To run amok because our brains are burning out.

Getting up. Walking around. Going into the kitchen, doing something with one's hands. Slicing bread. Chopping herbs. Standing in the middle of the kitchen, swinging one's arms, moving them in circles like a windmill. Jumping. Somebody calling my name from outside. Frau Umbreit, the fisherman's wife, stood at the door with an oblong package. You do like eel, don't you? But why don't you come in! ("Fish, storehouse for radioactivity!") We sat in the kitchen for a while. I received a detailed lecture on how to prepare sour eel, and Frau Umbreit was quite pleased that she had not yet told me the story of her fall through the cellar trapdoor five years earlier. How she had felt down there, she still remembered quite clearly. And then: a year in the hospital! Five operations! So I could understand her sometimes slightly unsteady gait, but I could still not understand how she came to marry a fisherman, with her aversion to fish. Oh, well. Where love strikes. But she had always cooked her husband his fish; he never had a reason to complain, and he liked it, too, it was perfect. Only, with some fish she can't even try the sauce, nor with venison, by the way. She just had her prejudices.

Then, after Frau Umbreit left, I began to chop up the eel, which twitched violently whenever I touched it with the knife. One of the headless, skinned pieces jumped off the table and performed a grotesque dance on the tiles. I got goose pimples all the way up my spine to the very roots of my hair. I said out loud: It's only their nerves!, took a rag, firmly grabbed hold of every eel and cut it up. Afterwards I could hardly pry open my set jaws. Then, following Frau Umbreit's instructions, I added so much vinegar to the water that it seemed almost too sour to me, as well as lots of onions, bay leaves, peppercorns, and salt, and placed the eel in a china bowl to cool. The whole kitchen reeked of fish and vinegar.

I took everything I intended to have for dinner out of the refrigerator, placed it on a tray, and went through the corridor, which was still very cold, and the entrance hall, passing by the calendar on my way to the big parlor. Never would I be able completely to express the sensations which were triggered in me by this walk through the dusky-green entrance hall, by the glance at a date. Is it worthwhile, brother, staking one's life on being able to express oneself ever more precisely, discernibly, unmistakably. Sometimes I am not embarrassed to ask such rhetorical questions, particularly when I'm not running a risk, since you have always reacted to them in a reliable way and will continue to do so. You will become determined and, displaying the pigheadedness from our childhood days, you will, should you deem it necessary, stand up for my obsessions, which are foreign to you, against me, being one of the few people who take me as I am.

(Nearly five months after that day which I am still

describing here, someone draws my attention to an item in the newspaper which I must have overlooked a few weeks back: a renowned young scientist had left the nuclear-weapons research center in Livermore upon terminating his contract. The newspaper is no longer to be found. I excitedly call the newsroom, a woman editor remembers the item, if not the name of the scientist, but promises to inquire into the matter. On the telephone the next day I hear precisely that name which I had not dared hope for: the man is called Peter Hagelstein. That can't be! I say. Yes, yes, it's right here, says the young editor. She must be surprised at my exuberance. Somebody made it. Nothing is final. I'll have to reconsider the destinies and decisions of modern Faust.)

The telephone again. My oldest daughter sounded tired, I still pounced on her with the question: What do you consider our blind spot? Oh, Mother! I asked her whether her answer would include the expression "living a lie." Not necessarily, she said, she would talk about that region of our soul, our perception, which remained in the dark because it was too painful for us to face. As a kind of self-protection, then, I said, and she confirmed this suspicion, an acquired protection against our own insights about ourselves and outside attacks. Whether, in her opinion, one should nonetheless endeavor to penetrate to our blind spot. In your profession? she said. Absolutely. But one couldn't go it alone. As we continued talking, I simultaneously compared my absoluteness at her age with her absoluteness and wondered whether at all she was still able to, or willing to, believe in my former propensity toward absoluteness, while asking her where she would set the boundaries in the experiment of dismantling our protective boundaries, and she answered as I had expected: There was no boundary, no stopping, once one had seriously begun. Depression? I said. Danger of suicide? These would reveal themselves as nothing other than forms of defense, tormenting to be sure, but still easier to bear than the concrete perception of one's true inadequacy. And once one had let them in, the depressing pressure would relent and the courage to act would grow—a painful process, to be sure, but also a pleasurably exciting one. Oh, daughter, I said, may your words reverberate on God's eardrum. You see, my oldest daughter said, now you're getting defensive again, and, as strongly aware as I was of the fact that a request for consideration is nothing other than defense, I felt compelled to deny her statement and abruptly drew her attention to the defense mechanisms of entire civilizations. That wasn't her department, she said, but why shouldn't there be a chance for an entire civilization if as many of its members as possible can dare to look their own truth in the eyes without fear? Which did not mean to burden the outside enemy with the threat, but to leave it where it belonged, in one's inner self. Whether this wasn't the most utopian of utopias, I asked myself, not her.

While we were still going over our experiences with

A Day's News

fear (don't generations differ, above all, in the objects of their fear?), my granddaughter came to the telephone. Yes, she said, so far everything was okay. Whether I knew Prince. A dog? I asked imprudently, and realized at that exact moment how I had once again provided testimony to my gaping ignorance. After the vehement reactions at the other end of the line had subsided, it transpired that Prince was a rock singer and looked like my granddaughter's new boyfriend. Or vice versa, I said, which she didn't hear. She had met Mike, the new boyfriend, at the disco the week before. He was cute. Blond or dark-haired? I asked. Dark, of course. Blond was simply out of the question. Never say never, I said, and heard my mother speaking through me; saw her standing there and heard her speaking on the telephone with her granddaughter, my daughter: Isn't it a bit early for all that, my child! So I didn't echo that sentence to my granddaughter, but listened to her emotion-packed comments about her various teachers, ever intent upon dividing my sympathies between her and the teachers, but my granddaughter had no use for a sense of justice, she was perfectly content with being sure of her likes and dislikes.

My goodness, I couldn't help blurting out, when my daughter got back on the phone. It all happens one or two years earlier now, doesn't it? They're in a hurry, that's why, she retorted. Perhaps something inside of them knows why. Is it a strain? I asked, and she said: Sometimes, for sure, and I drew her attention to the workings of retributive justice, which took an entire generation span to unfold. I then asked about my grandson. Whether they were able to keep him in the apartment these days. Out of the question, she replied. He raced around outside on his bike all day. But they had been showering him down thoroughly, and he would just have to stay inside if it rained. Incidentally, he was preoccupied with the ultimate questions of existence these days. Today, for example, sitting on the toilet, he had asked his father through the door: Dad, how come the big bathroom door fits in my little eye? Have mercy! I said. And? Naturally, his father had then made a precise drawing for him: the bathroom door, the eye, where the rays of light intersect, the path via the optic nerve to the visual center in the brain. And that it was the brain's job to enlarge the tiny reproduction in the receiver's consciousness back to normal bathroom-door size. And? Was he satisfied? You know him. Guess what he said? He said: But how can I be sure that my brain really gets the bathroom door back to the right size? Well, well, I said after a moment's pause. Hey, by the way: How can one be really sure? Will you just stop it! my oldest daughter reprimanded me, and then we spoke about how difficult they were finding it, especially now, after the long winter, not to eat the greens which were available at long last. We also spoke about you, brother, and I noticed that my daughter revealed the fears based on her professional knowledge more clearly to me, now, after the operation, than before.

A Day's News

I would have liked to say that I could do without her
consideration, but I suppressed the impulse, asking
myself in passing when it is exactly that the focus of
consideration shifts from the children to the parents,
and I would have liked to rebel against that as well.
Instead, I spontaneously asked my daughter whether
she still adhered to our once common belief that once
something had been said, it had been surmounted, or
whether she didn't consider that superstitious by now.
She did not answer that; I realized of my own accord
that we had probably never completely shared the
same belief in this matter, and I understood that she
was beyond those kinds of questions and did not want
to shock me with her more recent insights. Probably
could not believe that I would be capable of truly
accepting them. With a painful jolt, I once again
moved up a notch in the series of generations, the
sensation of being a fossil spread further within me,
the good old reptile within me gleefully slapped its
tail, or was it something dolphinlike, since toward
evening, having had my first sip of wine—Here's to
you, brother! To your health!—I entertain nearly all
manner of ideas; feel my self-censorship evaporate
with a sometimes almost wicked relief, also amusement, and so I yielded with that same amusement
to the fantasy that the dolphins—clever animals,
brother, whose brain mass in relation to their body
weight is not much less than ours—could once, in the
gray, distant past, have declined the gift of speech,
which may have been offered to them as well, upon

(97

mature consideration, in favor of retaining their whistling communication in the ultrasonic range, their playful existence, and their friendly behavior. For (this is what I realized on the evening of that day, the threshold of my inhibitions lowered, while I was alternately staring at different TV programs and eating, a folding table with my dinner tray set in front of the most comfortable armchair) we can try as hard as we like, we can stand on our heads and if it kills us: friendly we cannot be. We have accepted the gifts of false gods and all of us, every single one, have eaten the wrong food from the wrong plates.

But what does that mean, can any, even the most appropriate, formulation still have meaning, so much has already been said and written, the cordon of word nausea becoming ever denser, I never would have thought it possible, dear brother, for the time being I'm only telling this to you, growing older means: all that one would never have thought possible comes true, and how should I have foreseen that first the words, and then my words, would nauseate me, and how abruptly the turnabout into nausea at oneself can take place I wouldn't have thought either, so it is not true that one does not learn anything new as one grows older, he who bows out earlier has, no matter how hard the resistance may sometimes have been for him, only traversed the approaches, only now does he stand before the citadel, and in his darkest and truest hour he sees his own figure within, at which point one can no longer speak for fright, or for horror, one can no longer speak at all, for it may be calm at the center of the cyclone, but it is also silent (not quiet: silent, without a sound), plus and minus poles cancel each other out, "shame" may be a fine old word, and how I envy those who are permitted to renew themselves through shame, to whom purification through profession is granted, but it is no longer a question of renewal or purification, it is a question of total collapse and no promises at all, let alone an assurance for the time thereafter, apart from the one that there is no making amends, but, asks a vestige of resistance, must destruction and the desire to write be coupled, the circle of destruction surrounding a writer, how often have I observed it, how strongly feared it, sometimes managing to circumnavigate it, not always able to avoid it, since it appears to be in the nature of things, the essence of the vice of writing, that it knows no consideration and that the intervening writing process, so much talked about in the affirmative, always intervenes in the lives of people, persons who become affected by the writing, who are bound to feel observed, pinned down, categorized, misjudged or, worse still, betrayed, always kept at a distance, in any case, for the sake of an appropriate formulation, and for that I know no other remedy but silence, which transfers the ill from without to within, which means less consideration for oneself than for others, in other words, self-betrayal again.

The circle seemed to close, the cat bit its tail, I got a tight feeling in my chest, at which point my good old memory, which, after all, is sometimes my ally, drove a few lines my way, two verses of a poet from former times, and I had to change only one letter to break the ring:

You shall not plead excuse from me—you shall
Tell all just as it came!

Oh, well. Good old nineteenth century. "For me" or "from me"—and so is the entire difference contained in a single letter, and so, I thought, can one, no, must one be happy with language again after all. You shall tell all just as it came. I found the word "just" very amusing.

That evening they showed for the first time, on several TV channels, the silhouette of the accident reactor, an image which I expect will engrave itself in our consciousness just like that of the atomic mushroom cloud. They put some gentlemen in front of the cameras who, solely on account of their nicely tailored gray or bluish-gray suits, the matching ties, the matching haircuts, their prudent choice of words and the whole official capacity of their posture, radiated a soothing effect—quite in contrast to the handful of young, bearded, sweater-clad individuals who, on account of their agitated talk and manic gesticulations, aroused the suspicion that they had unlawfully commandeered the microphones, and I had to think of the people of the country, the silent, hardworking people of both countries whose gazes unite in the evening on the TV screen, and I realized: They will

take those in sweaters less seriously than those in their
suits made to measure, with their measured opinions
and their measured conduct; they want to sit back in
their armchairs after a hard day's work like me and
have their beer—wine in my case, what of it—and
they want to be presented with something that makes
them happy, a complicated murder plot, for example,
but nothing which affects them too much, and that is
the normal behavior we have been taught, so that it
would be unjust to reproach them for this behavior
merely because it contributes to our deaths. I, too,
sensed a strong inclination toward this normal behavior in myself, my wine was well chilled and gave
off a greenish glow when I held the glass up to the
lamp, and I felt good in my chair, in this room and
in the old house; you too, brother, would get well,
and why shouldn't a whole mass of other problems
find an amicable solution. So everything could have
stayed the way it was for a while longer as far as I
was concerned, and I, too, was listening to the TV
gentlemen in this secret hope. On the one channel
they were more preoccupied with the cloud, which
now also belonged to our large TV family in a small
way, the ragamuffin child, so to speak, and if I understood correctly, our cloud must have split in two at
some point, or it drifted off in one direction and back
in the other; in any case, Northern and Southern Europe were reprimanded for their regrettable levels of
radioactivity, but what could I do for the farmers who
swore wildly into the camera because no one could

tell them who was going to pay for the plowed-under lettuce; their money was their problem. My problem, on the other hand, was whether we, in an emergency such as this, had to consider ourselves part of Northern Europe, which we otherwise do, flippantly and, actually, out of vanity, or whether we do not, more precisely, belong to Central Europe. In the meantime, the gentlemen in the suits had enumerated to one another all those safety factors which exclude the possibility of a reactor accident and repeated to each other, and to us as well, all the reasons that seemingly make the so-called peaceful utilization of the atom indispensable—that was their word—and if one of them could not immediately come up with some argument, then another came to his aid; it was like a good lesson at school, and I was listening so attentively that after a few minutes I, for my part, was ready to whisper the answers to them, and I did it experimentally and was nearly always right. But then the moderator, who was interested in spreading a calm, composed atmosphere, thought he could safely pin down one of the two gentlemen to the statement that, even in this particularly progressive realm of science and technology, one could make absolutely faultless prognoses about the safety of the plants in question. But of course! I wanted to come to the aid of the interviewee, but that was hasty of me; for now the moderator and I were forced to learn, to our painful surprise, that this guy—despite his general willingness to be accommodating—was not about to be pinned down to this statement. Well, we heard him say, there was no such thing as an absolutely faultless prognosis in such a young branch of technology. As always with new technological developments, one would have to take certain risks into account until one fully mastered this technology as well. That was a law that also applied to the peaceful utilization of nuclear energy.

Now I should have grown cold. Now I should have been shocked or outraged. No such thing. I knew very well that they knew it. Only, I had not expected that they would also say it—be it only this one time. The text for a letter went through my mind in which I—imploringly, how else—was to communicate to someone that the risk of nuclear technology was not comparable to any other risk and that one absolutely had to renounce this technology if there was even the slightest element of uncertainty. I could not think of a real address for the letter in my mind, so I swore out loud and switched channels. I usually do not have the willpower, particularly not that evening, to switch off the TV. You can call this addiction, brother heart, and have done so with slight rebuke; I won't argue. To each his own button, as the rats have theirs, to each his weak point, through which the blessings of civilization can penetrate.

I had a choice of two films, both of which I already knew. In the older black-and-white movie, the actor playing Ingrid Bergman's husband attempted to drive her, his wife, crazy with flickering gaslights and other

such primitive apparitions. In the other one, an aging
officer in the English secret service, who is actually
already retired, succeeds, with the help of his good
old psychological methods, in exposing an agent from
the other side in the heart of his own headquarters.
In tasteful shades of brown, with time-tested actors.
I kept pressing the channel button and saw about half
of each film. The least of my worries that evening was
whether this continual flicking back and forth between channels makes for good mental training, or
whether it weakens the powers of concentration. I
was feeling superior to the agents of both world sys-
tems because they did not know and would not—for
a long time, perhaps too long—catch on to the fact
that their profession had become redundant. One,
two, three radioactive clouds from one, two, three
reactors in different parts of the world and the gov-
ernments would be forced to change their policies out
of the instinct for self-preservation, and proceed to
downright press their secrets upon the other side. But,
naturally, I did not delude myself into thinking that
it had already registered this evening with the em-
ployers of these nice agents that this radioactive cloud
had the capacity of letting one's adversary—or *adversaries*—vanish into thin air. That the sacrifice of
doing without the enemy was not the least of the
sacrifices which it categorically demanded of us. However, I wondered whether the simple instinct for self-
preservation can remain intact at all in people who

concentrate long enough on the destruction of the adversary . . .

I went to telephone one more time. In the evening as well the nurse—the night nurse by now—had made reassuring remarks to my sister-in-law concerning you, brother. No, you had in fact woken up, had been thirsty and been given a drink. How grateful I was to the nurse who had quenched your thirst. We reassured each other, talked a little about how we had spent this day, did not mention and did not want to know that you were feeling very poorly, that you were sick to your stomach and horrible pains had set in. I urged my sister-in-law, saying that it would be all right, to take a pill that night, to get some sleep for once. We still could not and would not say to each other all that we had imagined; which films had been running in our heads, in different versions, among them the one where the operation failed. We channeled all those flickering images to those areas of our brain where forgetting takes place . . .

I switched off the TV, locked the front, then the back door, did the supper dishes, put the cold cuts in the refrigerator. And discovered the parade of ants moving across the kitchen floor past the refrigerator, in a straight line, up the cupboard, heading with great determination across the marble surface for the tray with the jam jars. At last I knew how the ants got into the jam. So I had to liberate cupboard and kitchen floor from the ants, wiping them away, drowning them, crushing them, and sweeping them up and plugging, with a cottonball drenched in vinegar, the small hole in the rotten door frame out of which came marching the uninterrupted column. That would do for a few days. Then, luckily just in time, I remembered to fill buckets and pots with water, since, according to a public notice at the store, the water was going to be cut off for a few hours the following morning because of work at the pump house.

In the bathroom I forced myself to go through the same motions as every night, although I was so tired that I wanted only to sleep. Was I losing more hair than usual? What were the first symptoms, anyway? I still had to find a book in which to read a few pages to help me fall asleep. I suppose it was thanks to my tiredness that I took from the shelf the thin book by an author who had been urgently recommended to me for a long time but whom I still had not read because of my aversion to seafaring stories: Joseph Conrad. *Heart of Darkness*. I savored the first seconds of relief in bed, adjusted the position of the lamp above me, and, in a detached manner, read the first page, which, as expected, is about a ship. A seaworthy yawl by the name of *Nelly* which lies at the Thames estuary, waiting for the turn of the tide. Oh, well. I tried to picture the Thames estuary as I had once seen it, but the inner image was immediately pushed aside by a description of the evening light across the water which left me wide awake. "The day was ending in a serenity of still and exquisite brilliance"—this is how it starts. I read it twice. But then the narrator, whose name is Marlow, suddenly spoke the following sentence right to my face: "And this also has been one of the dark places of the earth." Finally, after all this time, I once again felt that thump against my heart which I feel only when a writer speaks to me from the depths of self-experience.

And this also has been one of the dark places of the earth. This also. And also this. I listened to the sounds of the night coming in through the open window, the quiet wind, the sleepy bark of a dog, and, for the first time this year, the frogs. I read on in tense expectation, and after only a few sentences I came to realize: yes, this Marlow knows what he is talking about. He has seen and understood it all, a hundred years prior to this, "our time," and here I lie and listen to him, frightened and delighted, speaking of the wilderness, of the deep darkness of the unknown continent, Africa, and of the secrets in the hearts of its inhabitants, to whom there is no path for the white conquerors. "Mind, none of us would feel exactly like this. What saves us is efficiency—the devotion to efficiency . . ." Ivory. Ivory, any amount of it, wrested from the wilderness and the savages, at any price and by any means, imaginable and unimaginable. Who can ever forget the old black man who gets beaten. Who the forest of death. Who the native village, its inhabitants scattered in mad terror: "What became of the hens I don't know either. I should think the cause of progress got them, anyhow." I groaned, for several reasons, among them in admiration for this writer. How he knew. How alone he must have been. And, on top of everything else, how can I bear to live with these six black men, forged together by chains. "They were called criminals, and the outraged law, like the bursting shells, had to come to them, an insoluble mystery from the sea." I could not read any further, not that evening. Leafing through, I picked out individual phrases, there they were: "Truth—truth stripped of its cloak of time." I would read on tomorrow, perhaps also find out which devices he used to such effect. How he managed to free himself from concepts such as "device," "effect"—the hardest thing of all. Enough for today. That writer, he knew the meaning of sorrow. He set out right into the heart of the blind spot of that culture to which he also belonged, and not in thought alone. Fearlessly into the heart of darkness. And he saw the light which must have led him too, on his way like a "running blaze on a plain, like a flash of lightning in the clouds."

We live in the flicker—may it last as long as the old earth keeps rolling.

So does this person speak to me. So shy, I could hardly expect to find words such as "hate" and "love" in his works. "Greed" I found, often. Greed, greed, greed . . .

Before falling asleep I saw that apparatus in intensive-care units which they call a "drip." Are you on a drip, brother? Are you asleep? Then a voice read me to sleep with the passage from the fairy tale in

which the true queen is turned into a duck. Now that
night the kitchen-boy saw a duck come swimming up
the drain, and it said: How now, lord king, art asleep
or waking . . .

Late at night I was startled by a voice and by a
crying. The voice had called from far away: A faultless
monster! The crying came from me, as I noticed after
quite some time. I was sitting in bed crying. My face
was flooded with tears. Just then, very close to me,
in my dream, a giant, nauseatingly putrescent moon
had swiftly sunk down below the horizon. A large
photograph of my dead mother had been fastened to
the dark night sky. I screamed.

How difficult it would be, brother, to take leave of
this earth.

June–September 1986

Translators' Notes

page

ix. *"The connection between murder and invention"* Carl Sagan, *The Dragons of Eden* (New York: Random House, 1977; London: Hodder and Stoughton, 1978).

ix. *"The long-sought missing link"* Konrad Lorenz, *On Aggression*. Translated by Marjorie Latzke (New York: Harcourt Brace Jovanovich, 1966; London: Methuen, 1967).

5. *"The Birds and the Test"* Title of a poem by Stephan Hermlin, who, like Bertolt Brecht, returned from exile to the newly founded German Democratic Republic. The poem refers to the influence of the hydrogen-bomb tests in the 1950s on migratory birds, which subsequently changed their traditional routes over the South Seas. Published in 1957.

5. *"In a clear brooklet . . . The wayward trout"* Franz Schubert, Op. 32.

8. *"In shadows cool and clean / Upon your carpets green"* German folk song.

9. *"O heavens' radiant azure"* Our translation of the first line of the refrain from Brecht's early poem "Ballad of the Pirates," written in 1918, first published in 1923 in the collection *Die Hauspostille*. John Willett's translation reads: "Oh heavenly sky of streaming blue!"—cf. John Willett and Ralph Manheim, eds., *Bertolt Brecht:*

Poems (London: Eyre Methuen, 1976). We have decided on a more literal translation for what are, we hope, obvious reasons.

9. *"Hurrying clouds like the ships of the sky"* Friedrich Schiller, *Maria Stuart*, III, 1, in *Five German Tragedies*. Translated by F. J. Lamport (Harmondsworth: Penguin, 1969).

16. *"O milk of inhuman kindness, bitter potion"* Last line of Stephan Hermlin's poem "The Milk," which is part of the collection that includes "The Birds and the Test." The preface reads: "Scientists have discovered that strontium 90, introduced into the human organism via radioactive milk, causes leukemia" (our translation). Hermlin parodies Schiller's line, the "milk of human kindness"— cf. *Wilhelm Tell*, IV, 3, in Schiller, *Wilhelm Tell*. Translated by Sidney E. Kaplan (New York: Barron's Educational Series, Inc., 1954).

17. *"Me Punch"* Punch must serve here as the nearest cultural equivalent to the German Kasper—a compromise at best, since the nature of Punch and Judy is much closer to that of the French Guignol. The eponymous hero of *Kasperletheater* is a "good guy" who battles against the forces of evil as represented by the devil and the witch.

27. *"Aghast, the mothers search the sky"* Our translation of lines from Brecht's poem "1940," from the *Steffin Collection* (1938–40). Sammy McLean's translation reads: "Mothers stand and humbly search / The skies for the inventions of learned men"–cf. John Willett.

27. *"what holds nature together there at its innermost core"* A paraphrase of Faust's monologue (I, Night). The lines read: "I'll learn what holds the world togeher / There at its innermost core"—cf. *Goethe's Faust*, Part I. Translated by Randall Jarrell (New York: Farrar, Straus and Giroux, 1976).

37. *"Marvellous Nature Shining on Me!"* First line of the early Goethe poem "May Song" (1771) from the Storm and Stress period. This translation is Christopher Middleton's, in Goethe, *Selected Poems*. Translated by Michael Hamburger, David Luke, Christopher Middleton, John Frederick Nims, Vernon Watkins (New York: Suhrkamp, 1983; London: John Calder, 1983).

39. *"It's raining / It's pouring"* The nearest English equivalent to the popular German nursery rhyme "Es regnet, Gott segnet . . ." This

Notes

was deemed more in keeping with Wolf's original, as a literal translation of the German would read: "It's raining / God blesses us / The earth is getting wet / The children rejoice / And so does the grass."

45. *"Man in the Holocene"* Title of a work by Max Frisch, published in 1979. Translated by Geoffrey Skelton (New York: Harcourt Brace Jovanovich, 1980; London: Eyre Methuen, 1980).

52. *"My eyes dwelt long upon"* From Brecht's poem "Remembering Marie A.," written in 1920, published in 1924. Translated by John Willett—cf. John Willett.

56. *"Thy Shrine we tread, Thou Maid Divine."* Beethoven's "Ode to Joy." Text by Friedrich Schiller.

71. *"How fares my child / how fares my fawn"* From Grimm's fairy tale "Little Brother and Little Sister," in *The Brothers Grimm: Popular Folk Tales.* Newly translated by Brian Alderson (London: Victor Gollancz Ltd., 1978).

82. *"When the sun sets we are able to perceive the stars"* Carl Sagan, *The Dragons of Eden.*

83. *"But in the social plight of our age"* Charlotte Wolff, *Hindsight* (London: Quartet, 1980).

86. *"Sweet evening sun"* Song by Anna Barbara Urner (1788).

100. *"You shall not plead excuse from me"* A paraphrase of lines from Friedrich Hebbel's tragedy *Gyges and His Ring* (1856), IV, 1450–51. Wolf has changed the original—"Du sollst *mich* nicht entschuldigen, du sollst nur sagen wie es kam"—substituting the reflexive pronoun *dich* for *mich*, a change of one letter, which she refers to in the text. We have substituted the preposition *from* for *for* in L. H. Allen's translation (London: Dent, Dutton, 1915), thus retaining both the approximate meaning and the integral wordplay of the original.

106. *"The day was ending in a serenity of still and exquisite brilliance"* From Joseph Conrad's *Heart of Darkness.*

109. *"Now that night the kitchen-boy saw a duck"* From Grimm's fairy tale "The Three Little Men in the Wood."